A CONSPIRACY
OF STRANGERS

LEE MARTIN

St. Martin's Press
New York

Design by Amy Ruth Bernstein

Library of Congress Cataloging in Publication Data

Martin, Lee, 1943–
    A conspiracy of strangers.
    I. Title.
PS3563.A7249C6   1986   813'.54   86-11378
ISBN 0-312-16433-5

First Edition

10 9 8 7 6 5 4 3 2 1

The plot of this book is fiction. At the time that I began writing it, I did not know that any such event had ever occurred anywhere, and in fact I was rather hesitant to write it for fear of giving someone ideas. It was only as I neared the end of writing that I became aware that in several other locations (not in Fort Worth at all) women had in fact been murdered for the reason given here. This story is based on no such real case, and any resemblance to any real person or event is completely coincidental and unintentional.

But I really do feel I should congratulate the two Houston detectives who spent over five years doggedly following small clues to break one such case. I'm glad I didn't know about their case in time; I might have been tempted to use it.

□ 1 □

I WASN'T THINKING about murder, that late September afternoon. I was watching my dog and wondering why I'd never noticed before that he ran sideways. His left front paw and his right rear paw line up, so that he always seems about to veer into something.

Somebody I mentioned that to later told me all dogs run like that. I don't know. I never paid much attention to dogs until the big brown mutt wandered in last Saint Patrick's Day, dirty and thin, wearing an old flea collar and an expired rabies tag. We fed him. We washed him. We fed him again. We put an ad in the paper—FOUND DOG—for all the good that didn't do.

Then we took him to the vet. There's a rabies epidemic going on among the skunks in this northeast corner of Fort Worth, Texas, and as far out in the country as we live, it would be very easy for a dog—especially a not-too-bright and overfriendly dog—to tangle with a skunk. Clearly he'd have to have shots.

It was on the way home with me driving that my husband Harry commented, "Looks like we've got ourselves a dog." Looking at the sixty pounds of fur shivering in his lap—the dog clearly did not like shots—he added, "Hi, Pat."

"Pat?" I asked.

Harry looked at me pityingly. "Deb," he said, "when did we find him?"

That was when I began to learn about dogs.

Tired of wondering about Pat's gait, I began instead to wonder what had possessed a respectable grandmother like me to acquire a habit of running up and down the side of the road, wearing jogging shoes, a yellow sweatband, a Bell Helicopter sweatshirt, dark blue terry cloth trousers, and a dark blue terry cloth shirt-jacket, unzipped to allow easy access to the pistol I'm required to have on me all the time.

But I knew why I'd started jogging. At my age I was getting more and more sedentary, and I had started to put on weight. A fat-and-lazy cop can become a dead cop—real fast.

Even if she is a grandmother.

I did not want to become dead right now; I'd only recently become a grandmother. Also I was still a mother, a wife, and a human being. In, I suppose, inverse order of importance.

Pat shot past me and across the road, barking loudly and wagging from the shoulders back to make up for his almost total lack of a tail. I shouted at him, but he ignored me and dashed into a field across the road, where he marked a dead tree as his property and then resumed barking. He never tries to bite anybody, and he rarely actually barks at people, but he loves to bark for no reason at all. Harry says he has the soul of a teddy bear with an overturned bark box, despite the fact that the vet, who calls him a "good ol' dog," thinks he's probably half Doberman and half pit bull.

He makes a lousy guard dog. The only reason I take him jogging with me is because he cries when he's left at home. As well as when he's taken to the vet, and when he's given medicine, and when he doesn't get fed exactly on time—but then to prove he's not a sissy, he fights every other dog he meets except Daisy, a terrier half his size who lives next door, who would eat Pat if he messed with her.

I was still feeding him penicillin capsules for the infected leg resulting from last week's fight with the squirrel dog up the street. I had to wrap them in slices of cheese to get them down his throat. When I tried to hide one in a spoonful of Alpo, he carefully ate the Alpo from all around, leaving a naked blue capsule tidily in the middle of an otherwise bare beige plastic bowl.

Pat started barking again, suddenly and loudly. Hoping he hadn't found another dog to fight, I shouted at him again and then caught a glimpse of brown as he charged out of the field, across the road, through a yellow and brown mass of wild sunflowers, and down the ditch on the other side, into a concrete culvert. Belatedly deciding to hear me this time, he ran back up the bank, joyously planting two slimy front paws on my jacket and bringing with him a charnel stench from the mud at the bottom. I staggered back—I outweigh him by thirty-five pounds, but he's far stronger than I am—and he danced happily after me, offering another good whiff of whatever he'd had his paws in.

It was that second breath that told me, and I slithered gingerly down the embankment with Pat cavorting around me. Mentally I began to shift gears, to put myself into my professional stance, but I wasn't altogether feeling like a cop yet, and the unexpected sight caught at the pit of my stomach.

She had long brown hair, tangled in driftwood and half buried in mud. She had good teeth; that fact was more obvious than I liked it to be, because rodents—maybe raccoons, or an opossum or two—had eaten her lips and other soft tissue around her mouth. I couldn't tell her eye color because the eyes too were gone, the sockets clogged with pale tan mud. She'd been white, and she'd been young. There was really no more I could tell, except for the obvious fact that the now-bloated body had been crammed almost entirely inside the culvert. There was something familiar about her that nagged at the back of my mind, but I couldn't figure out yet what it was.

I tried to tell myself this one might have been an accident. There'd been a lot of rain this week, the aftermath of a hurricane that had swept into Houston. The ditch had been running full. She could have fallen in, been caught in the culvert along with the brushwood. That visible dent in her skull could have resulted from washing against the rim of the culvert—and damn it, if she'd just washed another forty feet or so, she'd have been out of the city of Fort Worth, on into Watauga, and all I'd have had to do was sit and watch while Watauga—with its approximately fourteen-person police department—tried to work the case.

And then I asked myself whom I was trying to kid. I knew whose case this was. She wasn't in Watauga and she wasn't accidentally dead. I've seen a lot of murders in over sixteen years on the Fort Worth Police Department, especially these last two years since I was assigned to the major case squad, and I had no doubt I was looking at murder again.

I knew she hadn't gotten a fractured skull from washing against the culvert, not when her head was upstream of the culvert. And if she'd been washed down the ditch, she'd have floated with her head downstream, because the head is the heaviest extremity. No, she'd been put here deliberately, at least a week ago, I thought.

I was reasoning ahead of my data again. This is my worst flaw as a cop; I'm well aware of it, and usually I try to guard against it. But in all my years of policing, this was the first time I myself, off duty, not answering a call, had found a corpse, and, ridiculously, I felt a little uncertain as to how to proceed. I'd have to call in first, I told myself, and wondered whether to go to the pay phones beside Stop and Go on Beach Street, or just to go over to one of the houses in Summerfields.

I decided to head for Stop and Go. No need to excite the citizenry yet; they'd be plenty agitated quite soon enough.

Pat, meanwhile, was gamboling about me, alternately barking in hopes of getting my attention and growling deep in his throat as he caught the scent of mortality. That was a smell he didn't understand and wanted to investigate. I would have to get him out of the way before he started pawing at the body.

No leash, of course. Pat doesn't like leashes, and I don't like being dragged by an eighty-pound dog—he'd fattened up a lot since March.

I lured him over to the closest speed limit sign and tied him to it with the drawstring of my jacket. Of course he instantly broke the drawstring. I should have known he would; I've seen him straighten the hook of a tie-down chain.

I needed to leave someone with the body, but there was nobody to leave. Or I needed to stay with the body and send someone else to the phone, but there was no one to send. Cars were passing on Saginaw-Watauga Road—excuse me, Great Western Parkway, which is a ridiculous name for a tertiary road like this one—but none of them had stopped to check on a small woman and a large dog in the ditch. I'd just as soon they didn't stop, and I knew the body wasn't going anywhere, but still . . .

"Damn," I said, and clambered out of the ditch and took off down the road, grateful now for the summer of jogging as well as for the fact that Pat will follow me anywhere. In March I'd have been winded by the time I'd gone half a block.

I called the station. The dispatcher said they'd send somebody. Somebody, I knew, meant uniform cars and detectives and a deputy medical examiner.

Detectives? The first detective on the scene was me. But I wasn't even on duty. I was scheduled off for three days, to make up for the Labor Day weekend I'd had to work. Captain Millner couldn't . . .

Oh yes Captain Millner could. And very probably would. Well, I certainly couldn't investigate a murder with a dog dancing around me. I called home, figuring Harry could come and get Pat.

Harry didn't answer the phone. Olead Baker, who is probably going to be my son-in-law when he and Becky get around to discussing the matter, did. He said Harry was doing something to a radio and Becky was doing something in the kitchen and Hal—my fifteen-year-old—was doing something to a bike tire. Olead, who had been helping Hal, said he would break away and come get the dog. He didn't sound very surprised I'd found a murder. But then we'd met over a murder last January; for all he knew, I might find them all the time.

I hoped Becky was cooking supper, as I rather suspected I wasn't going to have time to do it myself. I guessed Becky was probably making chocolate chip cookies for Olead's little brother. At least she usually claims they are for Olead's little brother.

Olead arrived before the first police car, fortunately, because Pat, for his own particular doggy reasons, detests uniforms and people in them. I wasn't sure how easy it would be to lure him into Olead's Ford van, as he associates riding in cars with going to the vet, but with some persuasion we convinced him the van was a truck rather than a car—he associates trucks with going camping—and finally he hopped in.

With Pat safely stowed and whining loudly, Olead asked diffidently, "Is it okay if I have a look?"

I shrugged. There wouldn't be any crime scene to mess up. I'd seen the ditch running bank to bank three days ago; that meant any physical evidence was long gone.

Taking my shrug for assent, Olead went through the solid mass of flowers down the clay bank, careless of slippery mud on his blue and white Adidases. I followed, a little more carefully.

He didn't vomit.

Rookies often do, at a sight like this. Olead was no policeman, rookie or otherwise, and he'd seen corpses before, but they hadn't looked like this. Or smelled like this; I couldn't imagine why somebody from the closest part of Summerfields Addition hadn't found the body long ago, by smell alone.

Olead stood, both hands in the pockets of his jeans, and looked somberly at the body half hidden by driftwood. The culvert was small, only about four feet wide; it had been put in because the road was narrow here and there'd been a continual problem with cars sliding off into the ditch in rainy weather. I thought she'd probably been shoved in head first from the downstream side by someone who didn't stay around long enough to realize her head necessarily protruded from one side if her feet were all the way in the other. I wondered how it had been done. The limp dead weight of a body isn't all that easy to handle, and the diameter of the culvert wasn't large enough for anybody to have crawled in to manhandle the body from inside.

Rigor mortis, I guessed. The body must have been stiff, to have been jammed straight in. In that case, she'd have been dead about a day, maybe a day and a half, before she was brought here. That was the only explanation I could think of. But why here? Why not just bury her? Sooner or later, she was sure to be found; kids play in this ditch all the time.

"Deb," said Olead, who'd had his head much closer to the culvert than I wanted to get mine. "Deb, she was pregnant."

"Bodies swell a lot when they're left like this," I told him. Someday Olead will know a lot more about corpses than I do, but at that time he was in the first month of his first year in medical school.

"She was pregnant," Olead said positively. "Come and look."

I am not fond of the smell of long-dead humanity, but I'd been in the ditch long enough that my olfactory nerves had about gone numb. I'd be smelling it again when I got away from it, but right now it wasn't too bad. I took a closer look.

He was right. She was pregnant. That was what gave her that haunting familiarity. I should have spotted the condition as soon as I saw her, but I hadn't, maybe because I hadn't gotten close enough or maybe because, as a new grandmother, I didn't want to see a pregnant woman dead in a ditch. But I was almost back into my cop stance now, and I was beginning to feel more normal until I looked closer and saw something that chilled even me. The fingers of her right hand were open, spread wide apart with sandy mud between the fingers, but the left hand was closed around the root of a sapling that grew from the bottom of the ditch. Closed in cadaveric spasm, not just rigor mortis. And cadaveric spasm means instant death. Usually instant violent death.

She hadn't been put here dead, as I had guessed. She'd died

here, died not fighting but hiding, trying to protect herself and her baby from someone who'd found her.

There was a plain gold wedding band on her hand, too narrow to hold any engraving at all, the kind that's sold for $29.95 from umpteen catalogs and discount stores. She was wearing yellow maternity shorts that looked K Mart, and a yellow smock top that looked homemade. No shoes at all. If there'd been a purse, which right now I was inclined to doubt, it had washed down the ditch.

"Deb?"

I looked around. Gary Hollister, the lieutenant in charge of both Homicide and the major case squad, hadn't been on duty either, but like me he lived nearby. He'd arrived in faded blue jeans, a belt buckle that spelled out his first name, and an embroidered blue chambray shirt. His hands were grimy.

Gary is nominally my boss, but in fact I take most of my orders from Captain Millner, head of the Criminal Investigation Division. "Hi," I said to Gary.

He looked pointedly at the civilian prowling around the opening of the culvert. "What's he doing there?"

"He's with me," I said. "He's Olead Baker."

"Oh," Gary said in a tone of voice Olead wouldn't have liked if he'd heard it. Gary had been home with the flu last January when Olead was arrested for murder, but of course he'd known about the case, and although another man was now securely on death row for those killings, Gary still regarded Olead with some wariness. "That doesn't tell me what he's doing there," he added.

"It's my fault," I said. "I told him he could—"

"Baker!" Gary shouted. "What the hell are you doing?"

Olead's head snapped around, his face startled. "Looking," he said.

"Well, get the hell out of there!"

His movements deliberately casual, Olead ambled away from the culvert, paused with his hands in his pockets, and stared directly in Gary's face. "Okay," he said, and turned to me. "I'll take the pooch home."

"Thank you."

Halfway up the embankment, Olead turned. "Pooch is not an accurate word for Pat, is it?"

"Uh-uh," I said.

"Mutt? Hound? Indeterminate member of a canid species?"

"Olead," I said, "take the dog home."

He grinned at Gary, said " 'Bye," and opened the car door.

"Gary, I told him he could—"

"And I told him he couldn't."

"The point is you should have yelled at me, not at him. He asked permission."

"So why'd you give it?"

"What's with you, Gary?" I kept my voice low-pitched; the uniform officers now up on the roadside didn't need to hear veterans quarreling. But this was unlike Gary Hollister; the red hair on his head was no indication of temper, and in fact he had a penchant for practical jokes and was more likely to laugh than swear at the worst of times.

"Oh, hell." He ran the fingers of his right hand through his sweaty hair. "Just, Phillip Ross was with me when the call came in."

"You were on duty?"

"Dressed like this? I was on call, working in the garden, with a walkie-talkie on my belt. Ross has managed to find out where I live and he was over there talking at me."

"Oh, shit."

"I wouldn't let him come with me. But—"

"But he'll follow you. Sure. This can't be . . ." I turned to look again at the corpse. "His wife's been missing for months. This one hasn't been dead for two weeks—probably not much over one."

"You know it, I know it." He glanced up at the roadbed, where a blue Mustang had stopped in the middle of the road, effectively blocking traffic both ways. "I don't know if he followed me or if he's got a scanner in his car. I told him not to come here, but I knew he would."

All right, I felt sorry for Phillip Ross. And Chris McGuire, and Randy Garcia, and Dan Goldberg. I hadn't been working the cases, not until last week when Wayne Carlsen's heart attack had temporarily reduced the major case squad from six people to five, but I'd known about them. We'd all known about them, and this week I'd been getting new printouts to read because all of a sudden the cases had become mine. Mine, until Wayne got back. If Wayne got back, which didn't look too hopeful right now.

It was certainly possible this corpse could have been made a corpse by whoever was responsible for whatever had happened to Joanna Ross, and Darlene McGuire, and Allie Garcia, and Barbara Goldberg, all of whom were young, pretty, pregnant, and missing. Missing from the parking lots of shopping malls in Fort Worth over the last four months.

But almost certainly this corpse wasn't going to be any of them, because all of them had been missing a whole lot longer than this woman had been dead.

Phillip Ross was shouting at a patrolman who was trying to stop him from plunging down into the ditch. A policewoman joined the patrolman, trying to sound soothing, but she was a rookie and her voice began to rise in response to his. "Let him come on down," I called, and Gary glared at me and then shrugged.

Phillip Ross, his plaid sport jacket open and his brown slacks snagging on the rough stems of the sunflowers, scrambled down the bank, sliding briefly when the soles of his brown leather shoes slipped in the mud. He headed for the culvert, stopping abruptly when he saw the body. I heard a catch in his breath before he started retching. It was a while before he could straighten up, and I said, "Mr. Ross?"

He stared at me, his eyes accusing, and I waited. And waited.

And then asked what he was waiting for me to ask. "Is it Joanna?"

"How in the hell should I know if it's Joanna?" His face was pale and sweaty, and I started wondering whether we ought to send for an ambulance. But then he straightened and said, a little more strongly, "How can anybody identify that? It's like Joanna. That's all I can say. It's like Joanna. But I don't know. I don't know. I don't know."

·2·

THE FIRST TWO YEARS I was a cop I thought cops didn't cry. I wasn't trying to be macho—it's about impossible to be macho anyway when you're five feet two and the mother of three children—it was just that I thought cops didn't cry. And for those two years I didn't cry, at work or at home.

Then one day we worked a hit-and-run. It was an unavoidable accident and the driver wouldn't have been charged if he'd just stopped, only he didn't stop, he kept on going, leaving in the street a part-Oriental two-year-old just the size, just the coloring, of Hal, the baby Harry and I fought so desperately to get admitted into the United States to be our son. I looked at that poor crushed body in the emergency room, before they transferred it into the morgue, and I watched somebody from Ident cutting a sample of the baby's hair for comparison with hair that might be found on the undercarriage of the car—if they ever found the car, which as it happens they didn't. A hospital guard who had crowded in behind us—I guessed he must have been about sixty-five or so—said, "The Lord giveth and the Lord taketh away. Blessed be the name of the Lord."

It didn't sound corny, not right then, but the ident tech looked up and said sharply, "Don't blame this one on the Lord."

The guard went back out into the hall and a traffic investigator finally arrived from the scene, so that we were free to go back onto patrol. I went back to the unit and got in the passenger's side because I knew I couldn't see to drive. After a while Clint Barrington—he was my partner that night; that was before he went over to the sheriff's office—got in on the driver's side and reached across in front of me and opened the glove box and handed me half a roll of toilet paper.

"What's that for?" I asked.

"To get it out of your system."

"What are you talking about?"

"Damn it, *cry!*" he shouted at me, and I drew up my knees and sat with my back to him, my feet on the seat, facing toward the door, and cried for forty-five minutes in the dark of the emergency room parking lot, with the butt of my .38 service revolver gouging me in the ribs and the handcuffs looped through my belt poking my back.

Finally I sniffed, "Cops don't cry."

"Whatever in the hell ever gave you that idea?"

I didn't exactly know, I told him. And for the rest of the night, as we drove up and down the darkened streets of Fort Worth, Clint told me things I hadn't learned in the two years that hadn't been as long as I'd thought they were. He told me cops have the highest divorce rate in the world. The highest suicide rate. He told me there aren't very many old cops; there aren't very many retired cops drawing pensions. He told me about cops arriving at accidents to find their own wives, their own children, dead; he told me about cops getting killed while their partners were taking unauthorized breaks. He told me old cops either get drunk or they get religion, and he asked me which I wanted. I told him I wasn't very crazy about either one. Then he said, "Deb, you gotta learn to bend or you'll break. Which is it going to be?"

I didn't answer, and he yelled, "Cops cry, damn it!"

For the next three weeks, every time we were in a group telling war stories, he adroitly turned the conversation the way he wanted it to go. I heard a lot of cops, veteran officers, twenty- and thirty-year men, talking about tears they'd shed in patrol cars, sitting on the steps of the emergency room, at home after the watch was over.

And finally I figured out what he meant. You learn to shift gears. You're cool at the crime scene because you have to be. But the emotion is there; it doesn't just go away. It's stored up and eventually you have to let it out—some way—or you forget how to feel at all.

And that isn't good, not if you're a mother. Or a father. Or a husband or a wife or any human being at all.

But you try your best not to feel while the crisis is going on. Because you can't work a case when you're crying.

So I wasn't crying, standing there in the ditch looking at the sunflowers rather than at the corpse. I wasn't crying, but I wanted to. The EMTs had arrived; Irene Loukas from Ident had arrived. The body had been photographed in situ and the EMTs, doing a lot of swearing and wearing gas masks (one of them vomited in his gas mask) had gotten the body out of the culvert. It was lying now in an unzipped black plastic body bag. Olsen from the medical examiner's office and Dr. Habib, the deputy medical examiner, were crawling around in the culvert—which was not a place I'd want to be.

I'd talked Ross out of watching while the EMTs were work- ing. He didn't need to see the kinds of things that happen when a body in advanced decomposition is moved—the limbs that fall off, the bones that suddenly protrude through rotted, fragile skin—but he'd come back into the ditch after it was out and had looked again at the body in the unzipped black plastic bag. He was facing away from it now, crying great racking sobs and saying over and over, "I don't know, I don't know, I don't know."

"When was your baby due, Mr. Ross?" I asked him.

He stared at me, suddenly quiet, and I started to repeat the question. He drew the back of his hand across his eyes like a

fretful child and said, "Sept—September fifteenth. It was—it—
it would be . . ."

He started to cry again.

September 15. Almost a week ago. She'd been dead maybe a
week or maybe a little more; it was hard to tell for sure. Decomposition had proceeded faster in the parts of the body wedged
inside the culvert than on the face and the hands, because of
the dampness and the buildup of heat. Yes, she could easily
have been nine months pregnant, carrying a baby due about
the time she died. Only in that case where would she have been
for the last two months?

"What did her wedding ring look like, Mr. Ross? Would she
be wearing any other rings?" All this would be on the reports.
But I didn't have the reports with me. Not when I was jogging.

"Oh—it was—I wanted to get her a better one for her birthday or for our anniversary. I could afford it now. But when we
got married I—I—"

"Okay. I just wanted to know—"

"I was a PFC. In the Army. We didn't—didn't have anything,
not anything. I'm a stockbroker now, I make a decent—but
then . . ."

"Uh-huh."

"I got it at Wards. It cost me thirty bucks. That was all I had,
thirty bucks. I had to borrow the license fee from my brother.
But she never would let me get her another. She wanted *that*
one. Because it was the one she got married with."

"Uh-huh. What does it—"

"Just a little plain thin gold band. With lines around the top
and bottom, I don't know what you'd call it, kind of beaded, like
shallow grooves parallel to the ring only beaded-looking, you
know what I mean?"

I knew what he meant. I wished I didn't know. It would be
easy enough to remind myself that if this wasn't Joanna Ross it
was somebody else—somebody else whose husband had bought
a thirty-dollar wedding ring at Wards or some place like that

because it was all he could afford, somebody else whose baby was due in September. But the thing was, it was Joanna Ross's husband who'd seen this grotesque mockery of what had been a woman.

I didn't want this to be Joanna Ross.

But I was afraid that, once again, life didn't care what I wanted.

"Who was her dentist, Mr. Ross?"

"She had good teeth."

If this was Joanna Ross, where in the hell had she been since she disappeared? That was what didn't make any sense to me at all. "Had she had any dental work done that you know about?" I was carrying on two conversations, the one with Ross and the one inside my head.

"Ted Cohen." He must have been carrying on two conversations too; this was the answer to an earlier question.

That helped; Ted, one of the medical examiner's consulting dentists, wouldn't spook at this sight, as many dentists very well might.

"When will you know?" he asked.

"Know?"

"If it's—"

"Oh. Maybe this afternoon, maybe tomorrow. I'll call you as soon as they tell us."

He turned to head back toward the road, and I asked, "What are you doing?"

"I'm going home," he said. "What else is there to do?"

□3□

A FEW MINUTES LATER Dr. Habib asked me where I was going. "Home," I told him. "What else is there to do?"

He shrugged and crawled back into the culvert. I didn't know what he was looking for and didn't ask; I knew he'd tell me when he was ready to. I just walked back up to the road, sunflowers scratching at my pants legs, and headed for home. Walking, not running. It was full dark now, with moon and stars obscured by thick clouds that were blowing in from the west, and the street lights around Summerfields Addition aren't all one could wish.

Of course there was a lot else to do. Dr. Habib knew it and I knew it; I'd have to start doing some of it very soon, and I'd have to leave instructions for the rest of it to get done. But I wasn't on duty. Maybe I'd get real, real lucky and this case wouldn't be assigned to me.

I knew better than that.

But I did need time to develop a strategy—which is a fancy way of saying I needed to think about what to do next. I might as well do it at home as anywhere else, and anyway I wasn't going into the office dressed like this unless I had to.

Harry was sitting in his recliner chair somnolently watching the news; he glanced up when I came in and said, "Sit down, Deb." Olead was sitting in my recliner chair holding the cat; I think I'll give him that cat for a wedding present. He got up, annoying the cat, who shook herself all over and stalked into the kitchen looking offended, and went and sat beside Becky, who was on the couch maternally watching Olead's two-year-old half brother play with crayons and a coloring book. What Jeffrey was doing with the crayons didn't seem to have much relationship with what was printed on the page, but I guessed that was okay. Jeffrey seemed to have discovered the color green.

Hal was nowhere in sight. Since Harry and I had MTV locked off our cable box, Hal had begun to spend a lot of time visiting friends. Harry had suggested we might as well unlock it, since he was watching it anyway, but I didn't want to abandon my principles. I'm convinced there's a link between those awful videos and the appalling rash of teenage suicides. On the other hand, maybe I'm just getting old.

"I'm thawing some hamburger in the microwave," Becky told me.

"I thought I left some in the refrigerator to thaw this morning," I said.

Olead looked embarrassed. "I ate it. This afternoon."

"A pound and a half of—"

"I was hungry. I'll get you some more," he added hastily. "Was what's his name, Hollister, very mad at you?"

"Uh-uh, more upset than mad. I'm going to shower before—"

The phone rang. Harry grabbed it, said "Yeah," and handed it to me.

"Do we have a Grace missing?" demanded Dr. Habib, very loudly in my ear.

"Not that I know of."

"Well, this one's wearing an ankle bracelet that says Grace on it."

"Then she's not Joanna."

"I don't know yet if she's Joanna or not. I just know she's got a—"

"Okay, I hear you. Where are you?"

"Over on Loop 820 about to—"

I can't get used to car phones. "I'll call you back later. Are you headed for your office?"

"Yeah."

Dr. Habib works in the very fine and well-equipped medical examiner's office off Camp Bowie Boulevard, right by T-Com, as the Texas College of Osteopathic Medicine is familiarly called. Olead, who passes it several times a day going to and from class, might be very surprised to know just how much advanced analytical gadgetry is contained in that unpretentious-looking brick building. I've toured the place, and I've gone over many times to watch autopsies. I didn't plan on watching this one. Dr. Habib would tell me anything I wanted to know.

So I told him I'd call him back later, after I had time to check, and I hung up. "Now what?" Harry asked.

"More of the same," I told him, and headed for the bedroom, to juggle the telephone while I started to undress. I told the dispatcher to check and see if we had any Grace missing and call me back and let me know. While I was waiting for his call, I finished undressing and got out the shampoo. That's where the smell always gets, in your hair. Somebody told me the hair shaft is hollow. Maybe that's true, I don't know, but what I do know is that the bad smells, the ones you want to get rid of fast, get in your hair and stay. The other place they stay is at the back of your throat. I still haven't figured out what to do about that. I've tried mouthwash and I've tried gargling and neither seems to do any good; after something like this I tend to wake up in the middle of the night not seeing it again, but smelling it again. And again, and again.

It was with me now, and the smell that hadn't bothered me too much outside in the cool evening was making me increasingly nauseated in the suddenly stuffy bedroom. I opened the window above the bed and put a peppermint in my mouth to see if that would help any.

The dispatcher called me back. We did not have a Grace missing. I didn't think we did.

I told him to check with TCIC—the Texas Crime Information Center—and see if anybody had a Grace missing. He said he would and asked if I wanted him to call me back again. I asked his name—we have too many dispatchers now for me to know them all by voice anymore—and he said he was Reuben Dakle. I remembered Reuben Dakle from past months. He's thorough. I told him I'd call him back later, after he'd had time to check.

I went and showered and washed my hair and brushed my teeth and used mouthwash and, for good measure, spread some lemon-scented facial goop I got last year from Avon over my face. That meant I couldn't talk on the phone for about ten minutes, until it dried and I got it off, but it also meant the lemon was, at least for the moment, deadening what of the smell I still hadn't gotten rid of.

But of course the phone rang. Reuben Dakle, who'd decided he didn't want to wait for me to call him, informed me that Denton had a Grace Williamson missing and he thought it could be the right one. Naturally I asked for a description.

W/F. Twenty-four years old. Five feet two inches, 120 pounds, brown and blue. LSW blue jeans and TWU sweatshirt, blue.

I asked about jewelry. Reuben said nobody seemed to know.

I asked if she was pregnant. Reuben said nobody had mentioned it if she was.

I said something on the general order of "Shit" and asked how long she'd been missing.

"Well," Reuben said, "she went missing in May."

May, and this was September. I said "Shit" again and told Reuben to see to it the printout got on my desk. He said he would.

I washed the lemon goop off my face and the telephone, and dressed again—yellow pantsuit, shoulder holster, canvas sandals with no stockings—and headed for the living room. Olead and Becky were making spaghetti and laughing a lot, and Harry was doing something to a ham radio. He'd been doing something to it for days. Hal was back, and lending a hand with the soldering iron. Jeffrey was playing with the cat, who was sitting still with her ears laid back and her tail all bottle-brushy. I said I'd be back after a while. Harry said, "It never rains but it pours," and I said "Shit" again and slammed the door hard as I went out into a night rapidly becoming chilly. The wind was up; it would rain before morning.

I knew what was wrong. It was simple—I wanted nothing at all to do with this case. For the first time in over fifteen years as a police officer, I was totally unable to feel objective about the case I was working on. I didn't want to clear the case because it was my job, or because it was a puzzle I could sink my teeth into, or—or at all, to be honest. I didn't know who was kidnapping pregnant women; I didn't know who had killed this pregnant woman; I didn't know—not for sure—that the same person or persons had been involved in both cases.

What I did know was that I felt toward whoever was doing it somewhat as I feel toward tarantulas. Now logically I know tarantulas are basically harmless arachnids. Unlike black widows, unlike brown recluses, they rarely bite people, and when they do, there is rarely more than a small sting as an aftermath. But I react to them with utter loathing. When I see one sitting in the middle of a sidewalk with all eight legs hanging off the block, I'll walk an extra mile to avoid it. In my car I deliberately run over them; when somebody asks me why, I explain that any spider whose legs I can count from a car which I am driving at fifty-five miles an hour is too darn big to live in the same neighborhood with me.

There's no logic to that. And it isn't really even a matter of fear. My reaction to them is a kind of sick disgust which has no rational basis at all that I can find except, perhaps, an illogical conviction that spiders should not have fur.

Unlike the big hairy spiders, the person doing this was dangerous. Dangerous and deadly. But my reaction to him, like my reaction to the tarantulas, was not based on logic. It was a feeling of utter loathing. I wanted nothing at all to do with him. I wanted him stopped, yes, it was essential to stop him, but I wanted somebody else to stop him. Somebody else. Not me. I was not afraid of him. He was no threat to me. I was not pregnant. I had never been pregnant; all three of my children are adopted. It was like . . .

When I read *Helter Skelter*, I was looking at the Manson killings as just homicide cases, until I reached the description of Sharon Tate, with her copy of *Let's Have Healthy Children* beside her, pleading with her killers to let her have her baby, not to hurt her baby. Then it was no longer just a case. I too had bought a copy of *Let's Have Healthy Children*, in hopeful anticipation of the pregnancies that never came, and I wept for that flesh-and-blood woman and the child murdered in her womb. Perhaps it's because I can't have children that I empathized so strongly, I don't know; maybe most women would feel the same way.

What I did know was that I was reacting to this killing as I reacted then. Anyone who could kill a woman and walk away to leave her baby to die inside of her, perhaps living for hours inside a corpse, wasn't a human being to me; he was a monster, the kind of monster I'd far rather let someone else deal with.

But the job of stopping him had fallen on me. It was my job, and regardless of loathing or logic, I had to figure out how to do it.

It was nearly nine-thirty when I let myself into my office. The major case squad works basically in the daytime; there were no lights on. I flipped the switch and looked at my desk. Dakle had been prompt. The printout from the state computer was there. So was a printout of the initial report from the patrolman who had arrived first at the scene in answer to my call.

I dictated my report into a tape recorder for someone to type later, and then I did what I should have done before starting the report. I called Denton, and talked to a Sergeant Mary Gonzales.

Denton is a college town. Denton is, in fact, a two-college town—North Texas State University, population about twenty thousand, and Texas Woman's University, population a little over eight thousand. Of course a lot of that is commuter, but even the on-campus numbers are large enough. The result is that the police department is larger than a town that size would otherwise need, and Denton tries hard to have enough female officers to cope with a much larger than usual female population in the age group most likely either to commit or to be victimized by crime.

Gonzales had experience.

Gonzales hadn't, of course, taken the missing report herself, but she readily located the case file. She agreed with me that anybody taking a missing report should know whether or not the subject was pregnant, and should ask about jewelry. But then she sighed and added, "On the other hand, if the person making the report didn't volunteer the information . . ."

I asked who had reported Williamson missing, and she told me it was one of the TWU professors. That was sufficiently unusual for me to ask more questions, and Gonzales, audibly shuffling papers, said, "Seems she was—is—a graduate student, working on a Ph.D. TA as well as a student. A TA—also called a teaching fellow—teaches a couple of classes per semester, under very nominal supervision."

"I know," I said.

"Okay, well, she just didn't show up for class one Monday. Her last class had been on a Thursday, so maybe she'd taken off for a long weekend and just not gotten back. But that was unlike her—she was steady and dependable, and this was the fourth semester she'd been teaching there. And on top of that it was almost exam time."

"Okay."

"So the professor—a Dr. Westheimer—called her apartment to see if she'd been taken ill. No answer. For the moment, Westheimer covered for her, so her students didn't get a walk. But when she still hadn't called in or reappeared by Tuesday, Westheimer got somebody from the PD to go over there and check on her."

"And?"

"And she wasn't there. Nothing missing, no signs of a struggle, she just wasn't there. I mean she could have just left anytime, but the thing is, she had this cat she was crazy about. An outdoors cat; it came in to eat and be petted, but it always went outdoors. No sandbox, in other words. Well, of course nobody could tell if the cat had been fed recently or not—it was a pretty fat cat—but its water dish was empty and there was cat shit all over the floor, like it had been locked indoors for quite a while."

"What about her car? Did it ever turn up?"

"No car. She walked everywhere."

"Public transportation? Had she left town maybe?"

"We checked everything. Nobody had seen her to remember. Not that that says anything, of course. As well you know."

As well I knew. She could have left on anything from a horse to a 727. "Married?"

"Report doesn't say, so apparently not. There's no next of kin—report says to contact Dr. Westheimer with any news."

"Okay," I said, "can you get with this Dr. Westheimer and find out if Williamson was pregnant, and see what you can find out about jewelry she might have been wearing?"

"It might take a day or two. Late registration is still going on, and you know how hard it is to get ahold of college people that time of year."

I didn't know actually, but I said I'd take her word for it and hope to hear from her soon. I called Dr. Habib and filled him in, and then I locked my desk.

It was nearly eleven-thirty when I got home. Olead's van, of course, was gone, and the lights were off in Becky's room and Hal's room, but the porch light was on and the front door was unlocked. Harry was sitting at the ham radio—this is a hobby he's taken up in the last eight months or so—saying "CQ Japan, CQ Japan." When he saw me, he turned loose of the power

mike and said, "Spaghetti and garlic bread are in the microwave, salad's in the fridge. How's it going?"

"Lousy," I said. "I don't think I want any supper."

"Deb," he said, "eat some supper."

"Harry—"

"Sit down. I'll heat it for you. I guess you've got to go in tomorrow?"

"I guess I do."

"So upshove the days off again?"

"Looks that way."

People like to kill each other at 2 A.M. If they haven't done it
by then, they tend to wait till after 5 A.M.—only once in my life
did I ever get a call to a homicide between 2:15 and 5:30 A.M.,
and that one turned out to have happened earlier than we'd
thought at first. But I remember the week while I was assigned
to Ident that the phone rang within five minutes one way or the
other of 2 A.M. three nights out of six with word of a shooting.
The third of those nights I opened one eye, looked at the clock,
picked up the receiver, and said, "Where's the corpse?"

Harry said I sure would have felt funny if that had been a
wrong number, and I told him if it had been, the culprit would
have deserved the shock for waking people up at that hour. But
of course it wasn't a wrong number; the unsurprised voice of
the dispatcher replied, "Laying in the middle of Berry Street."

I am long out of Ident, and the types of cases the major case
squad works don't often start at 2 A.M. But the phone was ring-
ing, only two hours after I'd finally gotten to sleep, and I got out
of bed and staggered across the room to answer it. I'd had to
move it away from the bedside table after the time I answered
in my sleep and never really woke up at all.

I didn't recognize the voice of this dispatcher, but I could
hear the official noises of the dispatch room in the background,
along with an uncharacteristically excited commotion.

"Everybody out," he told me. "Millner's orders. We got a bombing."

"We got a *what*?" I demanded incredulously, instantly wide awake.

"We got a bombing. Abortion clinic on Belknap."

"That's in Haltom City," I told him. I knew the place he was talking about. Some abortion clinics are new and highly advertised; some are part of general women's health clinics. This was neither; it was, as far as I knew, a one-man operation working in an old building that used to house some kind of diet clinic.

I'd thought it was out of my jurisdiction. I said so. Again.

"Sorry, it's four hundred yards into Fort Worth. FBI's on it too, but Millner says everybody out. Homicide and major case squads both."

"Fatalities? Injuries?"

"Don't know yet. But Millner says—"

"Everybody out. I heard you. Okay, I'm en route." I slammed open the closet door. Usually, on the off chance of middle-of-the-night call-outs, I get my clothes ready the night before. But I hadn't tonight because I'd gotten in so late and so tired. As I turned on the closet light, Harry sat up. "Deb? What've you got?"

I told him, and he said, "In Fort Worth?"

"We knew it was coming. It's been happening everywhere else." I sat down on the bed to tie my shoes.

"That doesn't mean we have to get it here."

"We usually do get stuff here, after a while, whatever it is." On second thought, I pitched the sneakers back into the closet and grabbed for my arson boots.

"The way I look at it is this," Harry said. "There's a right way to protest and there's a wrong way. And throwing bombs, well, it's damn sure not the right way."

"That's a very original observation."

"So it's two o'clock in the morning."

"But I consider terrorism of any kind utterly revolting," I agreed, pulling the second boot on. "When you think about how long I tried to get pregnant—well, naturally I don't like the thought of abortion much myself. But I don't like bombs either. Whoever threw it might be thinking he's doing right, but he sure didn't think about the law. Or about the firefighters who have to put out that blaze tonight. Or about the cops who might get killed trying to defuse—"

"I'm not arguing with you, Deb."

"Oh, I know it, but I just get so damn *mad* about this kind of thing, and . . . Oh, rats!" Cops do get mad—about useless waste of human life, about total disregard of human rights. Maybe that's why we're cops, because we do get mad. But I'd already had an ulcer once; I didn't need to be getting another one now.

I threw my jacket on over my shoulder holster, slammed out the door, and nearly tripped over Pat, who was asleep on the doorstep. Apologetically wagging his hindquarters, he escorted me to the car.

I could see the glow of the fire long before I got to it. Belknap was blocked off by both Fort Worth and Haltom City police cars, and a lot of people were milling around in night clothing in the misty rain outside the barricade. I gathered it had been necessary to evacuate the adjacent trailer court, and then I remembered, with a sick feeling in my stomach, that behind this trailer court was a small private hospital. And in front of the trailer court, right next door to the abortion clinic across twenty yards or so of gravel road, was a gasoline station. The clinic, if I remembered right, was an old wooden building, not brick or even asbestos siding. It must have gone up like a box of fire logs.

No wonder these roads were blocked off.

Somebody in a Haltom City police uniform tried to wave me onto a side street. I leaned out of my car window and said, "I'm Detective Ralston from Fort Worth. Let me through."

"Yeah, sure, lady. Clear the scene, we don't need no sightseers."

I dug my identification out of my purse. "I'm Detective

Ralston," I repeated. "Major case unit, Fort Worth Police Department."

"You sure as hell don't look like no cop I ever saw," he said without looking at my ID, and I asked, "What are you, a rent-a-cop?"

"A what?" His voice went up about an octave.

"Are you a regular officer, or an auxiliary?"

"Auxiliary," he said resentfully. "But I'm trying to—"

"I might have known. What's your name?"

"Jorgensen. Doug Jorgensen. What's it to—"

"Jorgensen, I've been a police officer nearly sixteen years. Now I've shown you my identification, and if I don't get on into that controlled area, your name will be mud. Is that clear?"

"Now look—"

"No, *you* look! Get the hell out of my way!" My self-control, usually very good, was cracking—I was tireder than anybody ought to be, and this was another case I didn't want to be involved in.

A quiet voice approaching the car asked, "What's the trouble, Jorgensen?"

"Oh, this broad keeps insisting she's a cop, and—"

"Did you ask for her identification?"

"Well, I—"

I stuck my head out of the car window again. "Mitchell, will you get this idiot out of my way? I showed him my ID."

"Hi, Deb. Jorgensen, let her through."

I hadn't the faintest idea what I was supposed to do when I got there.

It wasn't that the situation was entirely unexpected. We hadn't, up until now, had any abortion clinic bombings in Fort Worth, but the possibility was considered so far from remote that the higher echelons in the police and fire departments and the FBI had gotten together to draw up contingency plans. The contingency plans, of course, included questioning all possible witnesses. But the problem was that the contingency plans had sort of failed to take into account the fact that the bombing would most likely occur—as this one did—in the middle of the night. Or the fact that the potential witnesses would be this numerous.

I estimated that four hundred people had been evacuated from the trailer court. There weren't any other residential neighborhoods close enough to be threatened, and the hospital hadn't been evacuated yet, but somebody had to figure out what to do with all these people. We couldn't talk to them at night in the rain, and they had to have shelter. Churches? Schools? There was a high school not too far away, if we could get in touch with somebody to open it up.

But that was a civil defense problem. I could only hope civil defense had been notified.

Who were the *real* witnesses, if any? I guessed that was going to depend partly on whether the bomb had been set in the daytime or at night.

Victims? Had anybody been in the clinic when it blew?

Usually the bombers in other places made sure the buildings were scheduled to be empty. We couldn't be sure they'd done that here; besides that, scheduled emptiness is not always actual emptiness.

I finally spotted Captain Millner, standing with his arms folded across the chest of his raincoat. Gratefully I headed toward him, and he spotted me about the same time. "Deb," he shouted, "come on over here."

He was about as disheveled as I'd ever seen him. Usually he is clean, shaven, and in order, no matter what the hour of the day or night—he is six feet two and looks like a television cop except for his age—but tonight he was unshaven and wearing a khaki shirt, khaki pants that didn't look too clean, and a yellow rain slicker he must have used twenty-five years ago when he rode traffic.

"What've we got?" I asked him.

"A hell of a mess," he told me. "Dr. Kirk"—he nodded toward a tall, thin, blond man wearing a white jacket and talking excitedly with a fireman—"says there should be three people inside. A nurse, a nurse's aide, and a patient."

I looked toward the blazing hulk of what had been a dentist's office and then a diet clinic before being transformed into its present use, and said, "Oh, no."

"I think 'oh, no,'" Millner said. "And before you ask, no, we don't know for sure if anybody got out. Right now I doubt it, between you and me. The place had gas heat and gas sterilization units for the medical instruments. The fire marshal says it looks like the outside walls were doused with some kind of petrochemical and then it was hit with about four Molotov cocktails at once. The person who called it in said he could see somebody moving around inside, but there was no way—"

And then, with no warning at all, the doctor I was watching out of the corner of my eye backed slightly away from the fireman, glanced at the closest patrolman, and ran toward the building. "Oh, damn!" I yelled, and went after him. Millner looked around to see what I was doing and then followed me; as he is a foot taller than I am, it didn't take long for him to pass me. Two patrolmen posted just outside the ring of firemen and equipment ran interception, but it took all four of us to wrestle the doctor to the ground, and even then it wasn't easy.

But finally he quit struggling and the patrolmen let go and Millner and I let go and the doctor sat up, shook his head, and looked at the building. "That was stupid, wasn't it?" he asked hoarsely.

"That was stupid," I agreed.

"They're dead already, aren't they?"

"If they're in there, they're dead. I'm sorry, Dr. Kirk."

"That stupid woman," he said, and wiped his face with the back of his hand. "That bloody stupid, *stupid* damn woman. If she'd told me the truth, she'd have lost one day. That's all. Just one day. Course I'd have sent her somewhere else, but they'd have taken her. One day. Now . . ." He shook his head. "That's why we were in there, that's why we were all in there. Only I left. I left to go over to the hospital, to get her a room ready, to be sure the OR was ready, before I transferred her. That's why . . ."

With no warning at all, he began to cry, and I sat and held his hands and let him cry, hoarsely, painfully, until Millner could locate the EMTs. They led him away. There was no use using the ambulance; it wasn't five hundred yards to the hospital.

I returned to Millner, who quietly resumed his conversation as if it had never been interrupted. "There wasn't any way to get anybody out," he said. "You saw it yourself. Three windows, one door, and fire coming out of every one of them. Burglar bars. The fire department was here within three minutes of getting the call, and by the time they got here, nobody was moving. The place was—well, you see it. They still haven't managed to get anybody inside. Kirk got here just before you did."

"Captain, I can't work this."

"I know you can't, but—"

"That thing I've got—the cases that got handed over to me. You did know about the body this afternoon, yesterday afternoon I mean, didn't you?"

He rubbed the bridge of his nose. "Yeah, I know about that. No, you're not on the follow-up for this one. But tonight, all the people we've got to talk to, all the statements we've got to take fast before the memories start to fade, we needed everybody out. Everybody."

As he spoke, I could see one of the burglary squad stumbling in, coughing in a gust of smoke that blew his way.

"Captain, I need a task force for just what I've got."

"I know you do. We'll do the best we can. But Deb, we just don't have enough manpower. We had a task force set up earlier and it didn't do much good. They chased everything there was to chase until they ran it into the ground, and there just wasn't anything left to follow that hadn't been followed."

"I don't know how much good I'm going to be able to do either."

"We'll get you a task force. It'll probably be mostly from uniform division."

And that would be untrained help. But he was right. We just don't have the people. By IACP recommendations we're on the nose—almost exactly one sworn officer per five hundred citizens—but a lot of trouble from the rest of the metro area spills over into the smaller towns. We're all stretched pretty thin as a result.

Civil defense notified us that the high school was opened up. The evacuated people were shepherded into it, and the detectives went along too. We talked to them all. None of them had seen anything. Of course.

The hospital didn't have to be evacuated and the fire didn't spread to the gasoline station. The people from the gas company came and shut off the gas mains to the building, and after a while the fire department got the fire out. When the fire marshals got in to check—by then it was almost dawn—they found the expected three bodies inside. And that was about all they found. The gas mains, before they were shut off, had gone on feeding the fire, and the destruction was fairly complete.

Captain Millner told me not to come in until Monday unless somebody called me. He said until the body from the ditch was identified there was really nothing much for me to do anyway, and I was working too much overtime.

So I've been told.

Sometime Saturday afternoon Gonzales called me from Denton to tell me that Grace Williamson was definitely not pregnant and would have been wearing no jewelry.

So Grace Williamson was still missing, still Denton's problem. And the Grace—if her name was Grace—who was dead in a ditch in the northeast corner of Fort Worth was still unidentified. There was no other Grace reported missing anywhere in the state, so far as we had been able to determine.

So I went back to bed, where I had been since I got home at nearly 9 A.M., and I slept until 7 P.M., when I got up and went in the kitchen and cooked supper for Harry and me. Hal had gone to spend the night with a school friend, and Becky and Olead had gone out—hard to believe that two years ago Olead was still in a mental hospital being treated for a schizophrenia that may or may not have ever existed, harder still to remember that only six months ago he had been on trial for murder. He hadn't committed the murders, and his doctor doubted now that he had ever had schizophrenia.

Harry offered to take me to a cafeteria, but I said I was too tired to dress; I'd rather make hamburgers or something like that requiring absolutely no thinking. Besides that I had to eat *fast*. Lately I'd been showing an alarming tendency to get sick every time I got hungry. I'd really have to see the doctor about that when I got time. I remembered those symptoms very well from the last time I had an ulcer.

We had hamburgers and potato chips and Cokes and watched TV, only I don't remember what we saw, until the ten o'clock news came on with a story about the bombing—they'd been talking about that on news breaks sporadically as long as I'd been up—and then they had a bit about the woman I'd found dead. Captain Millner apparently had decided to release word about the ankle bracelet; either that, or someone in the coroner's office had leaked it.

She'd been in labor, the television station said, and I wondered if that was true and if so where they'd gotten the information.

And about thirty minutes later, as I was preparing to go back to bed again, the telephone rang.

□ 4 □

An unfamiliar but official-sounding voice—with dispatch room noise behind her—said, "A guy just called and said he wanted to talk to the detective investigating that woman's body. I got his name and phone number. You want it now or later?"

"Just a sec, let me get a pencil or something." I made writing motions at Harry, and he handed me a pen and his ham radio log.

The man's name was Burt Freeman. I called the telephone number he'd left.

"Freeman." A tired-sounding voice. I empathized at once—I was tired too, despite having supposedly rested all day.

"I'm Detective Deb Ralston. The dispatcher told me—"

"Yeah, you're working on that thing at Summerfields, that woman?"

"Yes, sir, I am."

"Well, I'm thinking it might be my cousin."

His cousin was Grace Golden. She was separated from her husband and living in a little duplex in Haltom City; she was expecting a baby the middle of September. She liked to run around in shorts and no shoes. Her car was an old clunker, but she got around some. He'd just called her apartment and nobody was there, and he hadn't seen her in a couple of weeks. He didn't know if she had an ankle bracelet, but he said it sounded like the kind of thing she'd wear. She wore a lot of cheap junk, he said.

I got her address and called Haltom City to check it out. A patrolman would try to make contact, and they'd notify me.

Harry turned the television off and said if atmospherics were right, he thought he'd try to talk to Chile tonight. I said I thought I'd go back to bed. "Why don't you go to bed?" Harry said.

"I think I'll do that."

"Sounds like a good idea. I think you ought to do that."

We both started to laugh, and the telephone rang again.

By the time I finally got to bed—at one-fifteen—I had four more possibles. Grace might be (but probably wasn't) Grace Donohue, eight months pregnant, who had stormed out of the house three weeks ago after a quarrel with her husband. He'd figured she'd gone to stay with a girlfriend, and he hadn't checked to see which one. She'd done it before and she always came back.

She might be (but probably wasn't) Grace Jordan, eight and a half months pregnant, single, who had left home five months ago announcing she was moving to Houston. She hadn't contacted her parents since leaving, but they'd assumed she was all right until now this thing . . .

She might be (but probably wasn't) Grace Carstairs, pregnant widow of a construction worker killed in an industrial accident, present whereabouts unknown, or at least unknown to her husband's supervisor.

She might be (but almost certainly wasn't) Grace Sanchez, who'd left town eight months ago with a guy from a traveling carnival, and her parents thought maybe if she was pregnant she'd be afraid to come home and tell them and they knew that awful man she was running around with was a murderer or something . . .

Grace Golden sounded most likely so far.

I went to bed.

Sunday morning found me feeling somewhat more rested, enough more so in fact that I was able to spot the hole in Captain Millner's logic. There wasn't anything much for me to do, he'd said, until the body was identified. Well, yes, but who was going to identify the body? It was my case.

If I didn't go on to the station and get to work, I'd feel guilty because I was neglecting my work, even if I was scheduled off, but if I did go in, I'd feel guilty because I was neglecting my family, who like to have me home once in a while. So either way I was going to feel like a rat. Feeling like a rat, I put on a dress and went with Hal to church. This is not something I often do, but Hal particularly wanted me to go because he had a new scoutmaster he wanted me to meet.

I got home from church to find Harry barbecuing in the backyard. Still feeling like a rat, I changed into jeans and a T-shirt and went out to watch him and make appropriate admiring noises. After a while I came in and made a salad. We finally ate dinner about two o'clock—my older daughter Vicky, her husband the lawyer, and their four-month-old son Barry came over, as of course did Olead and Jeffrey—and finally, at three o'clock, feeling like a stuffed and sleepy rat, I put on a pantsuit and my holster and departed for the office, leaving behind a family watching the football game on television and not too likely to miss me until it came time for somebody to wash the dishes.

I called Dr. Habib to ask if he'd been able to identify the body. "This is Sunday afternoon," he told me somnolently.

"I know this is Sunday afternoon. Have you been able to—"

"It isn't Joanna Ross. But I could have told you that to start with."

"Why didn't you then?"

"Well, because I wasn't sure. You got anybody else for me to compare it with?"

"Not yet," I told him. Swearing, I dialed Phillip Ross's telephone number. He answered on the first ring; he must have been waiting beside the telephone, and I felt more like a rat than ever. This I should have done a long time ago. And would have if Habib had told me sooner.

I told him it wasn't Joanna, and he said, "Then where in the hell is Joanna?"

I didn't have an answer to that. He knew I didn't, and I managed to get off the phone with a minimum of awkwardness and get on to the next item of business. Which was the list of missing Graces.

I called Haltom City. They hadn't found Grace Golden yet. They had managed to get in touch with her mother, who lived in Garland, and she was on her way over. The dispatcher told me he'd tried to call me at home to ask if I wanted to meet her at the house and my husband had said I'd already left. Mrs. Murray was due to arrive around four-thirty. I said I'd meet them at Grace's house, and asked to have somebody make sure Mrs. Murray didn't get inside the house until I'd gotten there to walk through with her.

Four-thirty, and it was three forty-five now. I could work about forty-five minutes before I needed to head for Haltom City.

I called Grace Donohue's house; her husband answered, yawning, and said he didn't really think my Grace was his Grace; he'd just called because the neighbors were bugging him so. "Why don't you think so?" I asked.

"Ah, she's done this ten times before, took off and gone to stay with her friends so's she can scare me. This time she can stay gone for all I care."

"I understand she's pregnant?"

"Yeah, she's pregnant—damned if I know if the brat's mine or not."

"Oh?" I said.

"Yeah. Well, she said it was, when she was trying to talk me into marrying her, but she been running around with Mack and Donnie before me, and . . ."

"Yeah?"

□37□

"Well, she was real pretty before she got so fat, so I didn't care if I married her, but now she's so fat—"

"Mr. Donohue," I said, "pregnant women usually—"

"Not that," he said. "I mean she's up to three hundred pounds."

"Oh," I said lamely. "Oh, well, in that case she's not—"

"Your dead lady don't weigh three hundred pounds?"

"No, Mr. Donohue, she doesn't," I told him. "Thank you for your cooperation." I hung up and scratched Grace Donohue off my list.

Grace Jordan. Supposed to be in Houston. No job, no money—most likely I'd be able to trace her Monday by calling around to various welfare agencies. For now I put a great big question mark by her name and went on to Grace Carstairs.

Grace Carstairs had been reported missing, or at least semi-missing, by her husband's former boss—or should I say, by her late husband's boss. His name was Danny Kelly. Nice Irish name, I thought, and dialed the phone number he'd given me. A woman answered. "Mrs. Kelly?" I said.

"Yeah?" She sounded drowsy.

"I'm Detective Deb Ralston. Could I speak with Mr. Kelly, please?"

"What do you want to talk with him about?" Her voice had turned hostile, suspicious.

"He called me last night—"

"He called *you* last night? What about?"

It sounded to me as if Danny Kelly had a lovely married life. I said patiently, "Mrs. Kelly, I'm a police officer. Mr. Kelly called the police station last night in reference to a case I'm working on."

"You don't sound like no cop to me."

"Mrs. Kelly, I've been a police officer over fifteen years. I'd like to speak to Mr. Kelly. Of course if you prefer me to drive over there . . ." I can sound commanding when I want to, and I was beginning to want to. Apparently I succeeded, because I heard her shout, "Danny, come pick up the other phone. There's some lady that says she's a cop called."

Clicks and thuds. A heavy male voice said, "Yeah?" There was no sound of the other phone being hung up.

"Mr. Kelly?" I said. "I'm Detective Ralston. You called me last night about the body found in Summerfields. You suggested it might be Grace Carstairs."

"Yeah. So what?"

"I need to ask you a few more questions about her. Let's see, you told me her husband was killed in an industrial accident about three months ago, that right?"

"Yeah, that's right."

"Were they from around here?"

"Uh-uh. They were staying at some apartment on the south side, I don't remember exactly where now, but it was just a furnished place. He'd planned to move on as soon as the job was finished. You know a lotta these construction workers, they're like gypsies, can't stay in one place too long without getting antsy, you know what I mean."

"Do you know where she was from?" I asked.

"Well, not for sure, not unless she was from the same place as him. I mean, he could have picked her up any place he'd worked, you know what I mean. But he was from some little ol' town in Louisiana."

"Can you remember the name of it?"

"Yeah, just a minute, let me think, it was a real funny name." I could visualize him frowning at the telephone. "De Ridder, that was the name of it, De Ridder. Real funny name."

"And so far as you know she left Fort Worth after his death?"

"Yeah, it's just I figured she *might* . . ."

"I understand. Thank you again for calling, Mr. Kelly. I may need to talk to you again. Is that okay?"

"Yeah, sure. 'Bye." He hung up; I could visualize the jealous Mrs. Kelly steaming in the background.

I called the dispatcher next, to ask her to get in touch with the police department in De Ridder, Louisiana, and find out whether Grace Carstairs came from there and if so whether she'd gotten safely home again.

Thirty minutes left. I called the Sanchez household and got more of the same as I'd gotten last night, but in amongst the wealth of hysteria I did manage to garner a little information. Grace Sanchez had black hair. Grace Sanchez was four feet eleven inches tall. And the person Grace Sanchez had left with wasn't a carnival *worker;* he was the *owner* of the carnival.

I assured Mrs. Sanchez the body was not her daughter. Thinking Grace Sanchez might be well out of an overprotective home situation, I hung up and looked again at my watch. Then I said, "The hell with it," and drove out to Haltom City, to the little frame house occupied by Grace Golden—who was looking like an increasingly good bet as the body in the ditch.

It was lucky I'd left earlier than planned. The Haltom City police officer wasn't there yet, but Mrs. Murray arrived about the same time I did. She was a dignified-looking woman, dressed in a navy blue dress with a white belt and shoes. The shoes were an unfortunate choice, as the bare dirt yard was still muddy from yesterday's rain, but I supposed she'd wanted to assure the police that *she* at least was a substantial citizen regardless of her daughter's behavior. I could understand the motives.

She didn't tell me I didn't look like a police officer; that was a pleasant change. She merely produced the key and let me into the house. I hesitated; I had no legal right there. Texas has some nice new court decisions and laws that make it illegal to search a crime scene without a search warrant. Furthermore, I had no legal probable cause to assume this *was* a crime scene.

"Mrs. Ralston," Mrs. Murray said impatiently, "I pay the rent on this apartment. My daughter has never been able to hold a job and she certainly is in no condition to do so at this time. As I pay the rent, I have the right to invite you in. Please come in."

It might or might not hold up in court, but right now identifying the body was top priority. I entered, to find a scene of—not violence, but what seemed to be the aftermath of a large party. There was a couch, two lounge chairs, a small television sitting on top of a large console stereo. There were five beer cans and six Coke cans on the coffee table, and every available surface held an assortment of cans, bottles, glasses, and empty plates. A dried-up half of a peanut butter sandwich sat on top of the television set, an open bag of potato chips was on the coffee table along with three stereo records out of their jackets, and an end table held an open bag of Fritos and a lamp with its shade askew.

Mrs. Murray sighed. "She's not a very good housekeeper," she remarked, and led me into the kitchen.

A pan with chocolate chip cookies stuck to it sat on the stove on top of a frying pan which smelled of old grease. On the table were an open bag of flour, an open bottle of vanilla, an open can of Crisco, an empty chocolate chip sack, an open box of baking powder, an open box of baking soda, two eggshells, a white plastic box containing ten eggs, a bowl containing dried-up cookie dough, and three spoons. On the counter was a plugged-in coffeepot smelling of very stale coffee, a plugged-in mixer with some unidentifiable substance (probably cookie dough) dried on its blades, a blender (not plugged in) with something dried inside it, and a large bowl of brown salad surrounded by fruit flies. There was a bowl of apples that were rapidly turning brown, and two black bananas lay beside it. There too the fruit flies swarmed. The sink was full of cold gray water and an unidentifiable assortment of dishes.

The bedroom had a double bed with its sheets and blanket thrown on the floor, an old dresser with all three drawers partly open and underwear hanging out, a closet without a door with an assortment of not-very-clean clothes in it, and a floor that was virtually invisible due to the clothes tossed casually on it. In one corner of the room was a crib, new, made up with clean yellow sheets. In it sat neatly folded clean baby clothes, many of them still in their plastic wrappers, and under it was a pristine yellow diaper pail.

There were no newspapers. There was nothing to give a clue to how long she'd been gone.

"Does she have a car?" I asked.

"Yes, it's a 1975 Plymouth Valiant, light blue."

"Where does she keep it?"

"Out in front of the house," Mrs. Murray said. "Right about where you're parked."

She wasn't having hysterics. She wasn't saying, "Oh, do you really think it *is* Grace?" She was calmly providing the necessary information.

"Do you know the plate number?"

She told me the plate number, and I reached for the phone and then stopped myself. "I'm going to go use the radio in my car," I said. "Please don't touch anything while I'm gone."

"I'll just walk out there with you," she said.

And she stood beside the car while I put a lookout on Grace Golden's Valiant, without much hope of finding it. The cars of the other pregnant women who'd been kidnapped all had been reported the nights of the kidnappings; they'd all been left sitting in the parking lots of the shopping malls from which the women had been taken. An invisible place in the daytime, but an awfully conspicuous one at night.

Until a few months ago it would have been a conspicuous place on Sunday, but the blue law—the Sunday closing law—is gone.

Most of the stores close at six on Sunday, though, and it would soon be six o'clock. But she'd been gone at least two days, according to her cousin. The car, if it was at a shopping mall, should already have been spotted and reported as abandoned. It hadn't been yet.

Eventually somebody would have to photograph and fingerprint this house. That would be an exercise in futility, because there was no reason whatsoever to assume she'd been taken from here, but at least it could provide us with what would probably be Grace's fingerprints, to compare with the corpse. And of course it was routine. You do the routine things because they're routine and because sometimes they work, never because this time they'll work for sure.

"You don't want me to tidy up, do you?" Mrs. Murray asked.

"No, not now." I hated to ask, but it had to be done. "Do you suppose you could tell me her dentist's name?"

"She went to a dentist not far from here—let's see, it was across the street from the Catholic church. He had a funny name, now, what was it?" We went back in the house, and she looked through the telephone book and produced a name and a telephone number.

I promised to call her when we knew something, and she got in her car and drove off. No crying, no silly questions, no demands that I produce information I patently did not have. A very sensible woman. I wondered what kind of work she did, and then I went back to my office.

The dentist's name was Stoermer. I called the number listed and of course got a recording telling me the office hours. At the end of the recording, as I had hoped, was a telephone number to call in case of emergency. Calling that number, I got a crisp female voice that just had to be an answering service; she brightly informed me the doctor was not on call, and in case of emergency I should call Dr. Montgomery.

"Are you the answering service?" I asked.

"Hold please." In a moment she came back and assured me that she was indeed the answering service.

"I'm a police officer," I told her, "and we urgently need to locate Dr. Stoermer. It's about one of his patients."

"Oh, dear," she said, "I really don't know where Dr. Stoermer is. Dr. Montgomery is on call this weekend."

"Does Dr. Montgomery have access to Dr. Stoermer's files?"

"Well, I really don't know, but Dr. Montgomery—"

"Can you give me Dr. Montgomery's home telephone number?"

"Oh, dear, I really can't do that, but—"

"Will you please have Dr. Montgomery call me?" I asked resignedly, and gave her the number of the detective bureau.

□43□

The phone rang in about ten minutes. Dr. Montgomery was perfectly cooperative, but he did not have access to Dr. Stoermer's files. Their offices were about two miles apart, and he and Dr. Stoermer covered for each other on alternate weekends. And, he was sorry to tell me, Dr. Stoermer had gone to Las Vegas and would be home—presumably the worse for wear—on a 3 A.M. flight. After which he would, again presumably, get several hours of sleep before wandering, bleary-eyed, into his office to face his eight-thirty appointments.

I'd thought of getting fingerprints from the house, but I hadn't thought to ask Mrs. Murray if Grace had ever been arrested. The hands seemed to be in good enough shape for fingerprints, and if they were—and if there were any prints on file—that could clear up the identity question immediately.

I would call Mrs. Murray to ask, but I knew she hadn't had time to get back to Garland yet.

I pulled out the files I'd set up on all the killings. We don't have case jackets per se anymore, now that everything is on computer, but I can't get used to working a case without papers to work with, to line up side by side. So I always make my own case files. I put in printouts of all the reports, and I put in all my personal notes as I go along, so that if anything happened to me, somebody else could pick up without having to redo everything I'd done. I wished Wayne Carlsen had done that, but he hadn't been in the major case squad long and apparently the thought hadn't occurred to him. All I had of his was his official reports. Probably I was retracing his steps—in fact, I knew I was, because as Captain Millner had told me, he'd had a task force set up. But the task force had been returned to other duties. We hadn't had anyone go missing in two months, and every lead he had turned up had been followed to a dead end.

Now I was starting over and I guessed I'd find my own dead ends.

Part of the problem, of course, was that we had no way of knowing for sure whether Grace—if she was Grace, and if she wasn't, why was she wearing an ankle bracelet that said she was?—was even part of this series at all. The other women, I reminded myself again, hadn't been found. She'd been left in a place where we were sure to find her. Why the difference, if the same person did it?

I began to fiddle with reports, comparing and collating, and by nine o'clock I had decided that from all I could tell so far, the only thing Joanna Ross, Darlene McGuire, Allie Garcia, and Barbara Goldberg had in common was the fact of pregnancy. Darlene was thirty-three, five feet seven, brown and blond. Allie was nineteen, five feet even, brown and black. Barbara was twenty-three, five feet four, brown and brown. Joanna and Darlene looked Anglo, Allie looked Mexican (Mayan, from her picture), and Barbara looked Semitic. Joanna and Allie had long hair, Darlene had a frizzy perm (the kind I call a cocker spaniel cut), and Barbara had fairly short hair and had just had it styled the day she went missing. Joanna's car was found at Northeast Mall, Allie's at Tandy Center, Darlene's and Barbara's at Hulen Mall. They hadn't gone to the same churches, shopped at the same stores, or used the same obstetricians or, for that matter, the same dentists.

Wayne had been thorough. For all the good it hadn't done.

The phone rang, and an apologetic male voice with dispatch noises in the background said, "Deb? They've found that Valiant you put the lookout on."

"Where?"

"Parked behind the steak house at Northeast Mall. There's a sort of a little alcove there, and—"

"I know the sort of little alcove. All right. What's its condition?"

"Well, the doors and windows were shut but unlocked."

"Tell the uniform car to stand by. I'm en route."

That's North Richland Hills police jurisdiction, I thought, driving out there. I hate having the metro area cut up into so many little towns, but that's the way it is, and you have to learn them all because, unless you're in hot pursuit, you can't cross a city line without asking for the cooperation of the local constabulary.

Maybe it was Richland Hills. I was a little vague. All I knew for sure was that it wasn't the city of Fort Worth, and outside the city limits of Fort Worth, I have no jurisdiction—absolutely none.

I drove into the back of the mall without paying any attention to the patches on the uniforms of the two young men who stood beside the parked Valiant. I introduced myself and turned my attention to the car. It was, as I had expected it to be, stone cold—it hadn't been driven in hours, probably not in days.

I did *not* have the right—yet—to open the car doors, and well did I know it. And I didn't want to touch the doors, because if she had been taken from here, there was an outside possibility whoever did it might have touched the car doors, although we had gotten no usable prints from the cars of any of the other victims. So without touching anything, I examined the outside of the car and saw, of course, nothing unusual except a lot of dirt and several stickers from rock radio stations.

Without touching anything I looked inside the car through the open windows as best I could and saw nothing except several dozen pop and beer cans, several dozen wrappers from hamburgers and boxes from Kentucky Fried Chicken, some clothes, and—

Wait a minute. Wait a minute. There was a black suede purse inside the car, lying on the right floorboard with what looked like ice cream spilled on the fringe.

Not very many women go off and leave their purses inside unlocked cars, not even women as careless as Grace Golden appeared to be.

That was enough. I asked the Hurst officers—Northeast Mall had turned out to be in Hurst—to call one of their detectives and get a search warrant for the inside of the car, and I asked permission to have one of our own lab crews come out to process it.

By ten o'clock Detective Ronnie Fugate from the Hurst Police

Department had arrived complete with search warrant; Bob Castle and Irene Loukas from the Fort Worth ident section were on hand. Bob and Irene dusted the car doors and windows and took pictures from the outside, and Ronnie and I opened the car doors, and a blue pickup truck pulled up beside us. A male voice shouted, "Hey, what's going on here?"

"Police business," Ronnie replied. "I'll ask you to move on."

A barefoot, shorts-clad, very pregnant blonde scrambled out of the passenger's side of the truck and demanded, "What the hell are you doing with my car?"

"She'd decided to go to Galveston for the weekend," I told Harry, "and her boyfriend had said he'd pick her up behind the mall. Seems he works there and was leaving straight from work. She hadn't bothered to tell anybody she was going because she didn't figure it was anybody else's business. She'd left her purse because she'd spilled a malt on it and decided to buy a new one."

"So now who's the corpse?" Harry asked.

"Harry, you ask the damnedest questions," I said, and burped. "If I don't get something to eat, I'm going to be sick."

"If you don't get your Tagamet prescription refilled, I'm going to kick your bottom. You want another ulcer?"

"I've probably already got one."

□5□

DUTCH VAN FLAGG HAD the tall blond doctor—Kirk, they'd told me his name was—in the major case office when I got in Monday morning. "No," the doctor was saying, "no, there's not usually anybody there at night or over the weekends. I told you that."

"Tell me again."

The doctor ran his hands through his hair. "Okay. Could we turn on a tape recorder, though? This is getting monotonous."

"Later," Dutch said. "Right now I want to make sure we've got everything straight."

Kirk shrugged. "Okay," he said, "this patient, the one that was in the building, came in late Friday afternoon."

"Uh-huh," Dutch said. "Don't you work by appointment?"

"Sometimes, well, usually, but I can work people in sometimes, and she said she was really in a bind. She had to leave on a business trip Monday morning and she was going to be on the road six weeks and she had—according to herself—just found out she was pregnant."

"Do you believe that?" Dutch interrupted.

Kirk grimaced. "She'd probably decided not to know it up till then, and finally realized she'd better admit it to herself. People are like that. I've known women to deny to themselves they were pregnant until they got into the delivery room; hell, I've seen one who insisted the baby wasn't hers because she couldn't possibly be pregnant. You think I'm kidding? I wish I was. Anyway—she was begging me to do something fast. Well, she wasn't a kid, she was grown up enough to know what she wanted to do, and finally I told her that if she hadn't eaten that day I could go ahead and schedule a late surgery, but she'd probably still be feeling rocky Sunday, and she probably should go on into the hospital to be sure she got enough rest. She said she didn't like hospitals and she'd pay extra if I just let her rest in the clinic. I talked it over with Hazel—that's—that was—my nurse, and then I told her, the patient, that I wouldn't charge any extra for my services, but I would have to ask her to pay overtime for the nurse and the aide. She said that wasn't a problem. I told her again we'd have serious trouble if she'd eaten that day, and she swore she hadn't."

"Were you expecting complications, having extra people stay in?" Dutch interrupted.

Kirk nodded. "It was a possibility. It's always a possibility. Nobody in his right mind performs any kind of surgery alone in a building. As it happened—yes. There were complications."

"What kind?" Dutch asked.

Kirk hesitated. Finally he said, slowly, "To start with, there was more bleeding than usual, and on top of that she was vomiting all over the place. I wish she hadn't come to me. I won't do an abortion if the patient is over three months—I just don't think it's safe, at least not except in the hospital with a full staff to back you up. And you can make some kind of estimate by examination, but it's not a sure thing. I got in and then found out she was at least a month farther along than she said she was. That makes a difference. And on top of that she was lying in her teeth about not eating. If she'd started vomiting as soon as I got the anesthetic started, I could have just canceled the surgery, but she didn't, she waited till I got half done and *then* started vomiting. So there I was past six o'clock at night with . . ." His hands gestured futilely in the air.

"With an emergency. So then what did you do?" Dutch asked.

"Told the nurse to give her a shot of Compazine. Used suction to be sure her airway was clear. And finished the surgery. You can't just stop in the middle. Then I made sure bleeding was under control and her vitals were okay, and then I left to—"

"Left?" Dutch asked softly. There was open hostility in his voice.

"Left. I had to—"

"We'll get back to that later. So you left. You couldn't tell how far along she was? Aren't you a doctor?"

"Of course I'm a doctor. I took her word for it and thought the difference was maybe some puffiness or something—that sometimes happens—or maybe there was a possibility of multiple birth or something like that—without getting into a whole lot of medical terminology that wouldn't mean anything to you. And I didn't leave to go to the country club; I didn't leave to go honky-tonking, Mr. Detective Van Flagg. I left to go over to the hospital and make rounds—that's part of my job. I have regular patients. Then I grabbed a bite at the hospital cafeteria, and then I went to take supper to Hazel and Daphne so they could eat while I checked on Rountree again."

"Who—"

Kirk sighed. "Hazel and Daphne are the nurse and the aide, okay? I've told you that about six times. Can you please remember it this time? Okay, and then I stayed with Rountree a while and I didn't like the way she was responding, so I went back over to the hospital to have them get a room ready for her and get the OR set up in case I needed it, and that's where I was when the bomb went off. Doing my job as a doctor and trying to care for my patient."

"But you went off and left a bleeding and comatose patient—"

"She wasn't bleeding and she wasn't comatose, and Hazel is a—Hazel was a very good nurse and I was five hundred yards away." He came to a sudden halt and looked at me. "Do I know you?"

"She's a police officer," Dutch said.

"She doesn't look like a police officer to me."

"I'm a police officer," I said, resisting the urge to ask him what he thought a police officer should look like. "You met me last night."

"Oh, yeah," he said, looking slightly embarrassed.

"Go on, Dr. Kirk, I'm not interrupting."

"Well, I knew Hazel and Daphne could handle anything that came up at least long enough to reach me and get me back over there."

"Okay," Dutch said, "we'll get back to that later if we need to. You said something about some phone calls."

"I said that while I was over at the hospital the first time, Hazel got a phone call from a woman who said she was my wife and told Hazel I'd said she could go on home."

"Just Hazel? Not Daphne?"

Kirk sighed again. He rather made a habit of that; the sighing wasn't involuntary. It seemed rather to be a way of making a statement without using words. "She didn't even *know* Hazel. She said, 'The doctor says the nurses can go on and leave now.' And then she hung up. So Hazel called Ruthie—"

"Ruthie?"

"My wife. And Ruthie, of course, told Hazel she didn't make the call. Hazel told me about it when I got back in. But—look, we get some funny phone calls every now and then. I didn't pay a whole lot of attention. Not then."

"So who made the phone call?"

"Detective Van Flagg, I told you—"

"You told me you never told your wife to make that call. I know. Your wife told me she didn't make it. Then who did?"

"How the hell should I know who did? I just told you we'd been getting funny phone calls. Look, these are *my* employees that were killed, and *my* property that was destroyed—"

"And your patient that was killed?"

Kirk, by now so angry he was clearly getting rattled, shouted, "Yeah! And my patient! And you're acting like—"

"Oh, hell," Dutch said, "go across the hall and tell the secretary I said get a statement from you. When she gets it typed, bring it back to me."

Kirk headed for the hall. "What's going on?" I asked Dutch. "It sounds to me like you're hassling him."

Dutch leaned back and put his feet on his desk. "Around ten o'clock last night—he says—somebody called the clinic. Whoever it was talked to Hazel Chapman, the nurse there, and claimed to be Dr. Kirk's wife and said Dr. Kirk had said the nurses could leave now—that was the way she put it, no names, just 'the nurses.' Kirk says his wife didn't make that call and he didn't authorize anyone else to make it. At a guess, I'd say whoever called didn't know there was a patient in the building and didn't know there was a nurse's aide there—just thought there were nurses in there taking inventory or something and that when they left, the building would be empty, as it usually is at night and on the weekend."

"Dutch, you're acting like you think this is an arson-for-hire, a profit thing. Surely you don't—"

Dutch glanced at the door. "Oh, I don't really think so."

"Then why are you leaning on him? Dutch, I saw him last night, and—"

"Oh, I know. I just don't like abortions."

"I don't either, but they're legal whether you like it or not. And you can't lean on a man just because you don't like the work he does."

"It's not just that. It's that building, that location. It—I don't know, it's just so sleazy-looking."

Dr. Kirk wasn't gone yet. Standing in the doorway, he said, "You want to know why I bought that building? Picked that location?"

Dutch looked at him. "You want to tell me?"

Kirk walked back into the room and sat down hard. "Yeah. I want to tell you. You don't like abortions. I heard you. That's a legitimate point of view. A lot of people don't like abortions. But they're legal now, and there are all the nice shiny clinics for the middle-class women and the upper-class women. But the lower-class women—the kind that are living in neighborhoods like the one that clinic was in—can't afford those nice shiny clinics. They don't even call to ask, because they are sure they can't. They still play cute little games with coat hangers and knitting needles. You ever been in an emergency room and seen a woman brought in bleeding to death with a coat hanger between her legs? Or green pus oozing out onto her sanitary pad and a temperature of 106 degrees? I just figured if the rich people could have 'em, the poor people should too. So I chose that location on purpose, and I chose that building on purpose, so I'd be accessible to the poor women. So I'd look affordable. So they wouldn't be afraid to come to me. You know something, Mr. Van Flagg? I don't like abortions either. I don't like doing them. I'm a doctor. I like to help people. I like to save lives. But, Mr. Van Flagg, another thing I don't like is injustice. And the way I see it, I am saving lives. Maybe they're not the lives you'd pick to save—maybe they're dirty, worthless women who walk around in faded plaid blouses and faded striped skirts and plastic sandals, who have bad breath because they never go to the dentist and stringy hair because they never go to the hairdresser, but, Mr. Van Flagg, they're human beings, and I don't think I have a right to call them worthless. They're lives. So I'm sorry you think my business looked sleazy. I made a decision. Maybe it was the wrong decision. If it was, that's between me and the Almighty. But it was my decision and I made it and I'm responsible for it. And now I'll go talk to your secretary."

We could hear his shoes hitting hard on the tiled floor as he crossed the hall.

"Well," Dutch said, "that's a point of view I never thought of. What's sauce for the goose is sauce for the . . ."

"Banty hen," I finished when he paused with a puzzled expression on his face. "Dutch, was he sure it was a woman who made the call?"

"He says so. Says Hazel didn't know Mrs. Kirk well but said the voice sounded vaguely familiar, enough so that she called Mrs. Kirk to check."

So there was at least one woman involved. That wasn't totally unexpected; other abortion clinic bombing conspiracies had included women. The bombings themselves were usually carried out by men, because a man is more likely than a woman to have been taught how to put a bomb together, but even so . . .

I wasn't 100 percent sure it hadn't been an all-woman crime. It wasn't likely. But it wasn't impossible.

I was glad it wasn't my case. The one I had was impossible enough. I left Dutch with it and returned to my own work.

By now I'd chased down enough of Wayne's notes to find out Wayne had done everything I could think of to do about the missing women. But I was stuck with the case from Friday night, and I was right back to where I'd started from, with one woman, in an advanced state of pregnancy, dead in a ditch with no identity and no apparent motive.

I called the medical examiner's office and asked if Dr. Habib's autopsy report—postmortem, I corrected myself; he doesn't like the term autopsy—was ready, and if so, when could I have it. Rose Sprague, the secretary, told me she was entering it on the computer right now and it'd be ready in about half an hour if I wanted to come over there and pick it up.

I wanted to.

I sat in a snack bar on Camp Bowie with a Coke, to read and try to think; the new police station, larger and more convenient, is just as much of a madhouse as the old one was when it comes to trying to find a quiet place to think.

Victim had been a white female, age about twenty, primipara. That, I remembered, meant this was her first baby. Height five feet two inches—my height—weight 155 pounds. Normal weight, Habib said in parentheses, was probably around 120— my weight. She'd been my size. A small woman. Hair brown, eyes unknown. She'd been healthy and well nourished, but she hadn't been in the sun much and she hadn't had enough exercise.

Cause of death was a crushing blow to the right temple from something small and hard, but not pointed; death had been virtually instantaneous.

Subject had been either in labor or about to go into labor at the time of death.

That was what the newsman had said; so he'd been right.

Numerous bruises and abrasions on feet; subject had apparently run or walked a long way recently without shoes, and she'd gotten a bad sunburn the last day of her life.

No signs of defense wounds on hands. She had not tried to fight back; probably she'd known it was useless.

All right, if she'd gone a long way on foot, then she'd been trying to escape something or someone fairly close to where she'd died—walking distance, anyway, and what the heck is "a long way on foot"? That depends on health, on energy level, on how far the person has been in the habit of walking. But she hadn't been getting enough exercise, Habib said, so she couldn't have walked too far, especially if she was in labor. The neighborhood—I got out a Fort Worth Mapsco. All right, from the place of death going east was almost entirely Watauga. Going west and south was city of Fort Worth, and going north was city of Fort Worth for a little ways until Beach Street feeds into Alta Vista Road and it becomes Tarrant County sheriff's jurisdiction for a while and then runs into Keller.

I went back into the office and called Watauga and Keller, and I called the sheriff's office and then our dispatcher.

Watauga and Keller, of course, said quite truthfully that they were shorthanded, but under the circumstances . . .

The sheriff's investigators were tickled to death to get into the case. They'd been feeling left out.

And the dispatcher I talked to said he'd find me a few patrolmen.

Door to door. There are a lot of little additions in that area, and a few big ones like Summerfields; there are a lot of isolated houses, dairy farms, truck farms, mobile homes where somebody wanted to get out on some acreage and raise a cow and a garden and a handful of kids.

There weren't many people home, and none of those who were home knew anything about somebody named Grace who was pregnant and might be missing. They assured us they'd seen about it on television, of course, but they didn't know nothing about it, and no, nobody had seen a pregnant lady in shorts and no shoes out walking around two weeks ago, or at least if they did, they didn't remember, and how did I expect them to remember anyway if it was two weeks ago.

I considered that question entirely justified.

I did get one possible. A hamburger stand called Golden Burger on Denton Highway had a mature and alert assistant manager who told me he had a very vague memory of a woman stopping in about a week and a half or two weeks ago, in shorts and barefoot, who fitted that description. She'd asked for a glass of water. She'd asked to use the telephone. Told where the pay phone was, she'd said she didn't have any money. They'd let her use the business phone. She'd tried to make a call; either the line was busy or the person wasn't there. She'd tried to make another call—this one collect—with the same results, and then she'd left.

The assistant manager, a man named Don Coles, remembered her because she'd looked so tired and upset. He'd asked her if he could take her somewhere, and she'd said, "I don't know where."

He didn't know where she'd gone from there. He did know she'd seemed scared and disoriented, and he'd wondered whether he ought to call the police. But Don Coles, who happened to be nineteen years old, had decided she was grown up; she could ask for help if she wanted it.

And he had other things on his mind and hadn't thought about her since, until I asked. And no, he couldn't begin to guess what day that had been.

I bought two Golden Burgers and took them home to eat, since I was so close anyway.

If she knew somebody was after her, I wondered, why didn't she just call the police? Anybody would know to do that. So maybe Coles hadn't seen the right woman—only how many pregnant women are walking around barefoot in September?

Well, I didn't know. There might be a lot of them. Taking long walks barefoot might be the newest wrinkle in prenatal exercise. Never having been pregnant limited my knowledge of such things. I could ask Vicky, of course, but Vicky was back at work and might not want to be called.

So of course I called her anyway. She is a secretary at an accounting firm downtown, and the accounting firm told me she was out to lunch.

I might have known. It was that time of day—my stomach was loudly and complainingly reminding me.

I ate and I worried.

I can't honestly say I had developed a theory. The theory had sort of sprung up in my head, like . . .

I remember once right after I started policing seeing an old detective sitting at his desk with a burglary report in front of him and a forged check from the burglarized business in a plastic sleeve in his hand. He sat for two hours, reading and rereading the report and looking at the check, and then he got up and went out the door and came back an hour later with Billy Joe Martin. After Billy Joe confessed, I asked him how he figured it out. "I don't know," he told me. "If he hadn't 'fessed up I'd of had to let him go. I didn't have anything to hold him on. It was just, one minute I didn't know who did it and the next minute I did."

My theory had grown like that. And the problem was, I didn't know whether it was a legitimate theory based on my police experience, or whether it was something that had grown in my head because of my own particular psychological makeup.

I ate ice. And I gloomed.

Harry, who as I may have mentioned is a test pilot for Bell

Helicopter and sometimes keeps odd working hours—though not as odd as mine—wandered in, looked at the hamburger wrappers, and asked, "Did you save any for me?"

"Of course not," I said. "How could I know you were coming home?"

"Same way I knew you were."

"Which is?"

"I drove into the driveway and saw your car. How's it going?"

"Lousy," I told him, as I frequently do, and as he frequently does, he replied, "Well, there's one detective in this family and it sure as hell ain't me." He ambled into the kitchen, opened the refrigerator door, got out a chunk of cheese, and looked at it musingly.

"I just wish I knew *why*," I said. "Even if I don't know who she is, I just wish I knew why they killed her." Curled over with my head on my knees, I heard Harry walk over beside me. "I think they killed her because she got away," I went on. "They'd have tried to get her back, of course, but if she was making too much noise and they couldn't shut her up and they couldn't get her back in the car, then they'd have to kill her."

"Huh?" Harry said, and I sat up and looked at him.

"All I can't figure out is why nobody at her home has missed her yet. I don't know—I guess if they hadn't killed her when they did, they probably would have later on, but they killed her where they did—when they did—because she got away and they couldn't shut her up or get her back again. Harry, does that make sense?"

"It might if I knew what you were talking about." My face must have showed my misery, because he wandered around behind me and began to rub my back. "Debbie, Debbie, Debbie," he said, and with him rubbing my back I forgot to remind him nobody is allowed to call me Debbie. "Sure it makes sense. If you say it makes sense, then it makes sense. Why wouldn't it?"

"I don't know. I just keep thinking—maybe it's because of how I *feel* that I see it that way; maybe that's not the real reason at all. But I keep thinking about what's in all the newspapers lately . . ."

Harry didn't say anything; he just went on rubbing my back for a minute, and then finally he said, "So what's in all the newspapers lately?" He walked around me and picked up the front page, discarded on the couch, and glanced at it. "Hijackings. Bombings. Kidnappings. Murders. World War III in the making. You name it. What do you mean, 'What's been in all the newspapers'?"

"All those and something more. Babies, Harry. Don't you see? Those women had just one thing in common. They were all pregnant. Now think about it. Sixteen years ago, when we were working on getting Hal, all the red tape and all—"

"Yeah, yeah, and they said we wouldn't have gotten him except we had two minority babies already and they could tell we were taking care of them all right. And we had to go through the State Department and—"

"All right, and that was sixteen years ago. Harry, there just aren't any babies anymore. People as desperate as we were then can't get babies anymore, not from anywhere at all. There were the Vietnamese babies for a while, but that source dried up, and now—"

"Yeah, and that ring that was supposed to be bringing in Mexican babies, I remember that," Harry said vaguely. "The people were paying five and ten thousand dollars and not getting—"

"Not getting babies," I agreed. "All right—Harry, I've been reading in the paper that when babies *are* available, foreign babies I mean, even doing it legally now costs five or six thousand dollars, and then the baby is likely to be sick and malnourished—there are people who'd be tickled to death to pay ten thousand dollars for a healthy white American baby. They'd think they were lucky to be able to. And I just keep thinking, anything that one person is willing to pay ten thousand dollars for, another person is willing to supply even if he has to kill to get it—and even if it's a baby. But I'm still not sure I'm right.

I'm too emotionally involved to think straight. I ought not to be working this case. They ought to put me on the bombing instead."

"And then you'd be even more emotionally involved. You're talking about sixteen years ago—I remember something else. There was a story in the paper about some girl that died from an illegal abortion, and I remember you cried for days. You kept saying, 'But she didn't have to do that—if she didn't want the baby she could have just given it to me.' I kept trying to tell you that she didn't even *know* you, and her problem wasn't she didn't want the baby, her problem was she didn't want to be pregnant."

"So I wasn't very logical."

"You don't tend to be logical where babies are involved."

"That's why I ought not to be working this case."

"Or the bombing either," Harry said. "But since when do you get to pick and choose your cases?"

"We don't. That's the problem. But you can see why I'm afraid to trust my judgment on—"

"Oh, I think you're right," Harry interrupted. "I wish I didn't, but I do. Remember a few years ago when that baby was kidnapped from one of the downtown hospitals?"

Of course I remembered. I'd been on the case. So had the Texas Rangers and the FBI and some private detective agencies (who'd worked for nothing for the sake of getting the baby back) and you name it, they'd been on the case. "Yes, I remember."

"That's what happens when a baby is kidnapped. But these weren't babies; they were—are—grown women. And it makes the front pages a few days, sure, but then—"

"Then the publicity is over," I said. "And the hue and cry dies down—and if the baby is sold on the black market, nobody even knows whether the kid that's missing is a girl or a boy, and if the mother never turns up again, nobody ever even knows . . ." I stopped.

"Nobody ever knows," Harry repeated. "And that's about the size of it. Deb, maybe you are wrong. But I don't think so."

"No, I don't either now," I said. "I think that's where the kidnap victims are going—I think they're locked up somewhere until their babies are born and then the babies are sold and the women are killed. I just keep thinking . . ." I stopped. "I say that a lot, don't I?"

"Yeah," Harry said.

"But I just keep thinking, four women missing that we know of plus this one that almost got away—that, to the kind of mind we're talking about, adds up to forty thousand dollars or more on the hoof; you can buy a lot of chains and locks and a lot of cheap, nourishing food and a midwife or maybe even a doctor for forty thousand dollars and still have a lot left over to play with."

"And that's just in Fort Worth," Harry said.

"Right. That's just the women that are missing from Fort Worth. I haven't checked Dallas, or Denton, or the mid-cities, or—but they've got to be holding them somewhere near here, Harry, because Grace—whoever she was—got to that ditch on foot."

"I guess you're right, that they're holding them somewhere near here," Harry agreed, "unless maybe she came from somewhere around here and got away right after they caught her. But I think I'd go with the first premise."

"That doesn't mean they can't be kidnapping them from other places too and bringing them here," I interrupted. "And it doesn't mean . . ." I picked up the telephone and called the helicopter barn and asked for a police helicopter to meet me at the closest airstrip, the little one just off Beach Street where Harry keeps his private plane, and I went up in the helicopter with a borrowed pair of binoculars.

The pilot was a Vietnam veteran about the same age as Harry and me; he'd been a police officer almost as long as I had, and he'd been on helicopter patrol almost the whole time. "Deb," he said, "if you'd tell me what you're looking for, I'd be glad to help you look."

"I don't know what I'm looking for," I told him. "I want everything in a fifteen-mile radius of the corner of Beach Street and Saginaw-Watauga Road—I mean Great Western Parkway. Slow and low."

He shrugged. "You got it. But I sure do wish I knew what you're looking for."

As I had told him, I didn't know. And he didn't know, and if we'd been looking right at it—as it developed some time later we had in fact been—we wouldn't have known it. So finally he put the helicopter down where I'd left my car and let me out, and he headed for "the barn," as he called it, to leave the helicopter there for the oncoming shift and go home himself.

It was after four o'clock, I was starving, and I hadn't the slightest idea what I was going to do next.

□ 6 □

THAT'S NOT QUITE TRUE, of course. I had an idea or two; they just weren't very good ones so far as I could tell right now. I did call Dispatch and ask to have a message put on TCIC asking for details on any disappearances, cleared or uncleared, of a pregnant woman in the last six months, and I told the dispatchers that the answers, if any, were to be put on my desk.

I had a few more ideas, but they were still ephemeral, too fleeting for me to catch and act on yet, and anyway I was off duty and uneasily aware that Captain Millner had jumped on me several times lately about working too much overtime. Not that he minded the city paying for it, he emphasized; his objection was that I was wearing myself out and a too-tired cop is an inefficient cop. And, too often, an unsafe cop.

At least he'd finally quit arguing with himself about whether or not a woman belonged on the major case squad. He'd been somewhat uneasy about that for a long time; in fact, he'd let me on the squad only because, as he told me just last month, he was afraid I'd file a lawsuit if he didn't. Actually I wouldn't have. I don't think of things like that.

But the fact remained that I was off duty, and if I didn't want my captain wrapped around my ears saying unfriendly things, I had better stay off duty—unless called, of course—until about seven-thirty in the morning.

So I went home and found Hal standing at the kitchen counter making a peanut butter and jelly sandwich. "Hi, Mom," he said, and headed for the back door.

"Hal," I called after him.

"Yeah?"

"Aren't you forgetting something?"

"What? Oh, you mean like the jelly?"

"Like the jelly," I said. "And like the peanut butter. And like the bread. And like your homework."

"I did my homework at school," he told me. "I didn't have much." He put the top on the jelly and put it back in the refrigerator. He put the top on the peanut butter and put it back in the pantry. He collected the little twisty thing from the bread wrapper and put it back on and put the bread on top of the microwave, which is where we keep the bread right now. "The counter looks kind of crumby, doesn't it?" he said solemnly.

"Yes, it does."

He got a dishcloth and began to mop the counter. "Hey, Mom," he said, scrubbing industriously, "how long does it take a lady to have a baby?"

"Different people different times—why?"

"Yeah?" He stared at me in amazement. "I thought it was always the same time."

"I'm not sure we're talking about the same thing," I said feebly. "Suppose you explain a little more what you're asking."

"Well, I mean Sammy told me his aunt has a baby that's two weeks old and a baby that's eight months old, and I said I don't think you can do that because I think Vicky was pregnant a year or something like that, and he said who's Vicky and I told him my sister, and he said well Vicky must be a cow because only cows are pregnant a year, and so I hit him."

"Vicky was not pregnant a year. Vicky was pregnant nine months, which is the usual length of time, and you should not go around hitting people."

"Well, I didn't hit him hard. I mean he just laughed when I

hit him. But, Mom, his aunt couldn't have a baby that's two weeks old and a baby that's eight months old, could she?"

"Not very likely," I said. "Well, let's see. If she had a baby and then she got pregnant again right off and the second was very premature, yes, I guess it could be possible, but just barely."

"Is a nine-pound baby premature? Because Sammy said the new baby weighed nine pounds. Or something like that. Maybe it was seven or something."

"There is a certain amount of difference between nine and seven, Hal."

"Well, I don't remember. It was something like that."

"A nine-pound baby is not premature. A seven-pound baby probably is not premature. That's very interesting . . . Hal, do you know Sammy's aunt's name?"

"Uh-uh. He calls her Aunt Chrissie."

"Do you suppose you could find out? Does she live around here?"

"Uh-uh. I mean I could find out, but she lives in Canada."

"She lives in Canada."

"Yeah. And she's a foster mother or something like that. What's a foster mother?"

"It means they're not her babies. And it means Sammy was pulling your leg. Don't worry about it."

"You mean she adopted them?"

"No, a foster mother looks after children when their real parents can't, but the real parents probably will be able to get them back later."

"Oh. I think I'm going to go hit Sammy again. Harder this time."

"I would prefer that you not hit Sammy."

"Why? You think he might hit me back?"

"Hal, you're being a turkey," I said, and he laughed and departed, leaving me wondering whether *he* was pulling *my* leg. He is, after all, almost sixteen.

I wasn't actually worried about him and Sammy fighting; they had been the best of friends for years. But he had given me something to think about—yes, indeed, he had given me something to think about, and I thought hard about it until six o'clock when Harry arrived, reminded me it was Monday, and asked me if I wanted to go play bingo.

Since Hal had called me at five forty-five and asked if he could go skating with Sammy if he promised to come home at nine-thirty and go straight to bed, I said I guessed I would go play bingo with Harry. And of course with the Elks.

So I went and sat in a densely smoke-filled hall attached to the elegant old mansion that had been converted to the Fort Worth Elks Lodge and played bingo while Harry wandered around and sold bingo cards and came every now and then to look over my shoulder to see if I was winning. Of course I did not win. I never win at bingo. But at halftime I very properly went with the other Elks' wives and sold candy and hot dogs and popcorn and nachos and Cokes and beer and coffee to the bingo players, and made change in my head until I was dizzy, and then I went to the restroom and threw up. I looked in my purse for antacids and found none, so I emerged from the restroom and got a very large Coke and three bags of potato chips to settle my stomach—I didn't say I was logical—and finally I got to go home and wash the smoke out of my hair sometime after ten o'clock. Hal, of course, was watching television in the living room when I arrived.

I did not get called out at 2 A.M. Or 3 A.M. or 4 A.M. or any other time. I got up at 6:15 when the alarm went off and went in the kitchen and made oatmeal for breakfast, which of course nobody ate—why do I make oatmeal anyway?—and I went to the police station, stopping on the way to buy a sausage and biscuit because I don't like oatmeal either.

There were several printouts on my desk.

Garland had lost Lucy Waters, eight months pregnant, in July. Plano had lost Katherine Irving, seven and a half months pregnant, in August. Denton had lost Elise Tarcher, eight months pregnant, in July. McKinney had lost Ruth Lewis, eight months pregnant, in August. Sherman had lost Mary Grace Hammond, eight months pregnant, on September 3. Dallas had lost Edwina Foherty, eight months pregnant, in June, and Carley McLain, eight and a half months pregnant, in August, and was wondering what was going on.

I didn't, at first, read past Sherman. Mary *Grace* Hammond? September 3? Had she gone by Mary, or had she gone by Grace?

I called Sherman and got the assistant chief of police. He said he thought he knew, but he didn't want to tell me wrong so he'd look up the report and call me back. He said he'd get back to me as soon as possible, because kidnappings in Sherman weren't exactly what you'd call ordinary and nobody was very happy about it.

The pattern. Somebody should have spotted the pattern a long time ago, only nobody had, because he'd spread it out, he'd hit different cities. That shouldn't have mattered, not that much. We should have spotted it from the newspapers if nothing else, only . . . Why bother to make excuses? We'd dropped the ball because we'd worked separately, we cops in north central and northeast Texas; we hadn't gotten together to compare notes as we should have done and as we usually do.

That wasn't the whole reason either, I supposed. Seven women scattered around plus four in Fort Worth. The four in Fort Worth all had husbands, very worried husbands, but of the remaining seven, four were listed not as kidnapped but only as missing, with the implication that the disappearance was voluntary. Lucy, for instance, was only sixteen and she'd been fighting like mad with her parents; it was perfectly plausible she'd run away. Katherine had a husband and a good job, but she'd just been laid off from the good job and she'd been plenty upset about it; she hadn't much wanted the baby to start with, according to her husband, who'd added that she didn't seem to want him much either lately. On top of that, her car still hadn't turned up. Plano had been treating it as a possible suicide with a missing body.

And the others—well, so it went.

Nobody, from what little I could tell from the printout, would be likely to be looking very hard for Mary Grace Hammond.

She was unmarried, she was twenty, and she had a record.

But Chief Ellis had called it a kidnapping, and he'd sounded angry. So at least they were taking it sort of seriously.

The telephone on my desk rang. "Ellis, Sherman," said a terse voice. "I was right. She went by Grace among her friends. Still Mary Grace at home, but that was about the only place."

"Give. All you've got. I think we've got her here."

"Alive?"

But then he answered his own question. "No, or you wouldn't be asking that way. Okay. She was twenty years old, turned twenty in July. She had a little record—mainly drunk and disorderly, nothing serious, no hooking or anything like that. She lived with an aunt. Her boyfriend—they were planning to get married—got arrested here a while back for burglary and he's down in Huntsville doing time; they were waiting the wedding till he got back. Obviously."

"Obviously," I agreed. "He's the father?"

"Presumably. At least the both of them agreed he was, so who am I to argue? Anyhow, she had settled down, was working in a day-care center up until a couple of months ago when the doctor told her she'd have to get off her feet and take it easy a little more. She was having a few problems."

"Before we go any farther," I suggested, "let's see what we can do to determine if we've both got the same Grace. Size?"

"Five two. 'Bout a hundred and forty-eight pounds when she went missing—had weighed about a hundred and twenty-five beforehand, but you know how that goes."

"That fits. Coloring?"

"Brown and blue."

"Hair was brown. We couldn't tell about the eyes."

"That bad?"

"That bad," I told him, and he said, "Damn."

And then he added, "Okay, let me give you what else I've got in the way of description. She wore a wedding ring—they weren't married, but she, well, she was a little shy, you know, and she felt like it looked better. No other jewelry except some damn little ankle bracelet."

"Bingo," I said. "It have her name on it?"

"Did what have her name on it?"

"The ankle bracelet."

"Oh," he said, "well, sort of. Not her whole name. It just said 'Grace.' The boyfriend give it to her."

"You got fingerprints on her?"

"We got fingerprints on her."

"You want to bring them here, or had I better come get them?"

"You still got the body? It hasn't been buried or anything?"

"We've still got the body."

"I'll bring the prints. I'd like to have a look at her. I think I'll recognize her."

I doubted it—I doubted that anybody could recognize her now—but I said that sounded okay to me, and it took him about two hours to drive down from Sherman, which was some very fast driving. But of course you're less likely to get a ticket if you're driving a marked car.

We left her fingerprint card with our ident people, who had succeeded in getting legible prints from three fingers, and Chief Ellis and I went over to the morgue. Dr. Habib seemed to be out of pocket, and there was no reason to involve the other pathologists; we got a morgue attendant to get the body out. Ellis looked at the body and said, "Well, I couldn't say for sure, but it sure as hell looks like Mary Grace to me. And I've been knowing her since she was six years old."

"She been in trouble that long?"

"Uh-uh. I live next door to her aunt."

"Oh," I said. There didn't seem to be much else to say.

He turned away, muttering, "I'da never figured that pretty little thang'd turn out this way," and I followed him out and shut the door, leaving the morgue attendant to put her away.

Dr. Habib stopped us in the hall.

"I thought you were out somewhere," I told him.

"I was just out for yogurt," he said. "Even MEs have to eat sometime."

"Dr. Habib, this is Assistant Chief Ellis from Sherman," I said. "We seem to have Grace identified."

"Visually?" He sounded dubious. I couldn't blame him.

"No, Bob's looking at her fingerprint card, but the anklet and all fit."

"Let me know for sure."

That was a silly thing to say. Of course we'd let him know for sure. He had to have the information to finish his reports, to say nothing of the death certificate.

When we got back into the police station, we went straight to Ident, where Bob Castle told us what we were already pretty sure of anyway. Our known Grace was Mary Grace Hammond, twenty years old, from Sherman, Texas. She'd been missing over three weeks before she was found dead—and by now Dr. Habib had told us she hadn't been dead much over a week before she was found.

Ergo—she'd been stored somewhere alive. And it was somewhere within walking distance of my house.

I called Dr. Habib and told him the name, and then Ellis and I sat down and talked about the case and about Grace. He showed me everything Sherman had on it; there were a few points that looked strange to me. I pointed them out to him, and he agreed they looked strange, and somehow without my quite noticing it was happening, it became decided that Wednesday morning I was going to go to Sherman to talk with Clara Hammond. She was the aunt—great-aunt, actually—who had raised Mary Grace Hammond.

I still had part of Tuesday afternoon left, and I still had the nebulous idea I'd been chasing Monday. I looked in the telephone book and called the county clerk's office and asked for information. The first person I talked with said she couldn't possibly help me, and she referred me to someone else, a John Christmas, who told me, in some surprise, that he had no information on how many babies a year are born in Tarrant County.

"Why don't you?" I asked. "Doesn't the county clerk's office keep that kind of record? It certainly used to."

"Used to, I'm afraid, is the operative term," he told me. "Each city keeps its own vital statistics. We keep records only for the unincorporated parts of Tarrant County."

"Huh?" I said. "When did this go into effect?"

"Oh, dear, it's been quite a long time ago. 1972, as I recall."

"1972?" Well, it was true that it had been longer than that since I had need of a birth certificate.

"Most likely," he continued, "the people to help you would be the Fort Worth office." He provided that number, and I called it. There I was told that approximately ten thousand births a year are recorded in Fort Worth.

That's just in the city of Fort Worth. It doesn't take into account the unincorporated areas, or the other little towns like Richland Hills and North Richland Hills and White Settlement and the parts of Arlington located in Tarrant County and . . .

I thanked him, hung up, and dug some Tylenol out of my desk. I had suddenly found I needed some.

Then I called Captain Millner and asked him if he'd gotten those patrol officers to help me yet. He said they were due to report in tomorrow morning. I told him I was going to be in Sherman tomorrow morning, and then I told him what I wanted them to start doing, and he said, "Deb, you are crazy."

He tells me that every now and then, when I get these bright ideas. Clint Barrington used to tell me the same thing. Sometimes the way the ideas work out gives me the feeling they just might be right. But most of the time the crazy ideas work. Well, sort of work. Well, sometimes I get some usable information from them.

This one, I had to admit, was a lulu. And I wasn't even sure what I was going to do with all the information once I had it gathered together.

It would help if I had a computer program to do it. Roddy Anderson, one of the city's computer programmers, is an old friend of mine. Briskly I gathered myself together and walked the six or so blocks to the city hall to talk to Roddy, who said, "Deb, you are crazy."

"Yeah, but can you *do* it?"

Roddy and I went to school together. We have known each other far longer than I should like to admit. He therefore feels privileged to talk to me as if he were my brother, which he now proceeded to do. "Yes, of course I can do it, but it is some more kind of a wacky idea. What do you think you're *doing*? I thought you were a cop, not a statistician. And who do you expect to enter all this information so that it can get sorted out?"

I told him I had borrowed three patrolmen, and he said, "Arrgh! Who's going to teach them to enter it?"

"Well, if you'd teach me, then I could—"

He growled again and told me he would make the program very user-friendly, and he would see what he could do about making terminals and computer space available, but, he asked, did I have any idea how long all this was going to *take*? I told him I thought the idea of a computer was to speed things up, and he said, "Oh, it will, it will, it's just that first you've got to get all the information *entered*. Deb, twenty thousand—"

I told him it wasn't going to be twenty thousand, and he said, "If it's ten thousand from Fort Worth alone, it's going to be at least another ten from the rest of the metroplex."

"Roddy, that's for a whole year," I protested. "I only want, let's see, March through September, seven months. Not quite even seven months really."

"Goody goody gumdrop, you only need to do twelve thousand instead of twenty thousand. That really does simplify all these entries."

"You don't have to sound like a Doberman."

"Like a *what*?"

"Like a Doberman. They always look so—so—dismayed, somehow."

"How did Dobermans get into this conversation?"

Trying to explain the Doberman expression on Pat's face would get too involved. "Never mind, I think I'm getting tired," I said. "Just, can you do it?"

"Yeah, Deb. Okay, let's see. Exactly how much information do you want for each entry?"

"Mother's name. Father's name. Date of birth. Place of birth. Name of obstetrician or midwife. That's not really too much, is it?"

"No. And you want it to sort by all of those things?"

"Uh-huh."

"Okay, here's how I'll set up the program," he said. "As I said, I'll make it as user-friendly as possible. That's what you need, right?"

"I guess so."

"Then it'll prompt. It'll number the entries. And for each entry it'll ask for each of those items and it won't go on to the next item until it gets either a name or 'unknown' for the item. That way your people can't get screwed up and get ahead of themselves. Really and truly, with no more than that it probably won't take as long to enter the information as it will to get it. I just don't know what you think you're going to get out of it, Deb."

"Roddy, I don't know what I'm going to get out of it. I don't know if I'll get anything out of it. I might just be wasting a lot of time and money. But I've got to try."

"I know, Deb. I know you've got to try." He grabbed a huge sheet of what looked vaguely like graph paper and began to write on it. "∅∅∅1.∅∅∅1" I saw before he looked over at me and said crossly, "Go away. I have to think."

So I went away. Despite Captain Millner's disclaimer, the city had lately become extremely antsy about police working overtime unless it was 100 percent unavoidable. Even if we offered to do it for nothing, no overtime pay, no comp time, nothing on the record at all, the city was antsy. And the lieutenants and captains had been known to wander around the building at 4 P.M. chasing everybody on day watch out.

I went home, ate supper, and took Hal to a Boy Scout meeting, wishing he'd found a troop closer than the 820-121 split, and wishing the troop sponsor was a church I felt more at home in. What, I wondered, was wrong with the Elks troop?

But he'd told me, firmly, that he didn't like it. And that I had to take his word for.

Clara Hammond moved slowly, as befitted a woman of, she told me proudly, eighty-three. She was a large woman, not just fat but big. She'd have been big even if she weren't fat. She had on gold-rimmed trifocals, and her teeth had that too-regular pearliness of old dentures, but her hair still had as much black as gray in it. Her ankles were thick, and both of them were wrapped in elastic bandages covered by support stockings. She leaned heavily on a black wooden cane. But quite clearly her age was only physical.

Her house was older than she was. Entering the small, cluttered front hall, I found myself looking up a dark staircase. Doors opened to my left and my right; the door to my right was propped ajar by an open unabridged dictionary, and the hall floor was littered with uneven stacks of books. Through the open door I could glimpse four walls of books and more stacks of books on the floor.

She led me through the door to the right, into a room crowded with rickety Victorian furniture. Chairs and love seats had arms and backs neatly spread with antimacassars, and on every available flat surface were small, framed photographs, mostly black and white; pieces of delicate old china jostled each other. "Sit down," she said, and I sat.

I'd had a great-aunt whose house had looked much like that one. I told her so. She didn't smile; she grunted and said, "I guess all old ladies' houses get to looking a lot alike."

My great-aunt, I told her, hadn't had *quite* so many books.

She grunted again. "Did you come here to talk about my house and my books, or about my grandniece?"

I told her I'd come to talk about Grace, and she said, "Then let's talk about Mary Grace. What do you want to know?"

"You've been—"

"Notified of her death? Yes, Sergeant—excuse me, *Chief*—Ellis told me about it last night. It's no more than I expected. She wouldn't have stayed gone three weeks without coming home or at least calling for money. I knew she was dead."

"She's been living with you—"

"Since her mother died, when she was six years old. And it would be easy for me to say Mary Grace was the way she was because of that rascal of a father of hers, but I can't say that.

The fact is Mary Grace is—was the way she was because of the decisions she made herself. But isn't that the way it usually is?"

I agreed that that is the way it usually is, and Clara Hammond sighed. "That's not what you want to hear. September third, that's what you want to hear. All right. It started before that, call it the last week in August. Mary Grace had been full of herself. She'd called that boyfriend of hers and they'd talked for a while and then she came in and told me she'd decided to let the baby be adopted out. That was the right decision, of course, and I'd been telling her so, but—she was excited. You could tell. She was really full of herself—did I already say that? Doesn't matter. She was excited. And she got two or three telephone calls here at the house and then she left here September third, early in the morning, and said she'd be back later."

"Did she drive, or was she on foot?"

"She was on foot. Sherman is a small town. There's not many places you can't go on foot."

I said I realized that, and Miss Hammond said, "Well, what else do you want me to say? She left and she didn't come back, that's all. She just—didn't come back."

"Did the police here search her room?"

"Why should they? She didn't go missing from home."

"No, but she might have written something down. Would you mind if I . . ."

Miss Hammond sighed again. "Miz Ralston," she said, "look at all these pictures. We were a real big family, once. But— things happen. It's hard to say how they happen. Just, somehow the real big family got littler and littler and littler, and then one day there was nobody left but Mary Grace and me. Now there's nobody left but me, and I'm eighty-three. Go and look in Mary Grace's room. It's at the top of the stairs on the right. Go and look all you want to and take anything that might help you. Because it doesn't matter much now."

□ 7 □

Grace's room was a hodgepodge of old furniture. Not antique, just old. I had a hunch everything of value in this house had long since been sold, to keep the old woman and the girl going. A three-quarter-size bed on a metal frame sat in the middle of the room, its headboard below an open window. It was unmade, a quilt turned back to display a blue blanket and a pair of blue sheets. Surprisingly the room, despite the clutter that resulted from too much stuff crammed into too little a space, was basically clean. And Grace had to have done the cleaning herself; I expected it had been years since Clara Hammond had been able to climb these stairs.

A cedar chest to the left of the bed served as bedside table. It had a dresser scarf embroidered with green-stemmed violets on it—how long had it been since I'd last seen an embroidered dresser scarf?—an old lamp, a digital clock with a couple of paperback romances standing neatly beside it, and a deck of playing cards in a plastic box serving as bookend. To the right of the bed was a keyhole dresser, six-drawered, with a round mirror held in an ornately carved stand. The dresser also had an embroidered dresser scarf on it; in the places the scarf didn't cover I could see the veneer was peeling off the underlying wood. Arranged more or less neatly were a hair brush, a comb, a set of hot rollers, a tube of Alberto mousse, a curling iron, a curling brush, and an assortment of cosmetics sitting on a mirror tray. A box of yellow Kleenex and a plastic jar full of multicolored cotton puffs jostled a box of Q-Tips she'd apparently used as eye shadow brushes.

Tucked behind the open bedroom door was a small, rickety desk. On top of it were envelopes, notebook, paper, another lamp, a Crystal Lite container holding pencils, and a telephone. There were three drawers down the left side, but no lap drawer.

With the vague feeling of guilt for snooping that always attacks me when I begin to search a victim's room—I have no such qualms when searching a suspect's room—I began to look methodically through the papers in and on the desk. She had a red address book; I took that. There was no desk calendar; she did have a wall calender from some service station tacked to the wall above the desk, and she seemed to have penciled dates and times onto it. I'd need it too.

There was no loose scratch paper on her desk, no notepads—most women find it impossible to conduct any kind of social life without something of that type sitting next to the telephone. There were a couple of felt-tip pens; she'd surely written on something with them, and it wasn't the calendar because what was written there was in pencil.

A stack of letters from the boyfriend in prison. I'd take those; she might have told him something, and if she had, he might have replied to it. I'd have to remember to ask Miss Hammond if any letters had come from him since Grace went missing—most likely there were some, and those I'd certainly need, since they'd probably comment on that last telephone call she'd made, and on any last letters she'd written him.

Nothing in the drawers except some rather innocuous reading material, an unopened box of dime store stationery, and a book of stamps. Nothing written. No names, no dates, no numbers.

She hadn't even had a record player.

In the dresser I found nothing but clothes, cosmetics, and souvenirs.

I moved the things from the top of the cedar chest and opened it. Nothing there except more clothes—mostly out-of-season nonmaternity clothes—and more souvenirs. I turned my attention to the very small closet and once again found nothing except clothes and shoes. Grace had made no provisions at all for the impending arrival of her baby; I wondered whether she might have decided she wasn't keeping it long before she told her aunt. If she had any plans at all to keep it herself, she'd waited somewhat long to lay in supplies—unless, of course, there was something in the other rooms.

Which I didn't, as yet, have permission to search.

I went back downstairs and asked, first, about the letters, and without saying anything Miss Hammond got up, crossed the room leaning on her cane, opened the drawer of a sideboard, and took out three letters. She handed them to me and began to return to her chair.

"Miss Hammond," I asked, "is there any possibility Grace could have been storing stuff—letters, papers, that kind of thing—in some of the other rooms in the house?"

"It's possible," she replied, "but I don't think she was. Look anywhere you want to. Except the bedroom downstairs; it's mine and I'd know it if she put anything there. I don't think she's been in the book room much, but you look all you want to. I don't have any secrets in this house, and if Grace did, well, she's dead."

I really didn't know what I thought I was looking for. But it did seem that Grace, unlike many, if not most, of the other women, had left willingly, apparently thinking she was making adoption arrangements. Not a very intelligent girl, I guessed, and certainly not an educated one; she probably had not even realized there was anything wrong with the prospect of receiving money—however much she had expected to receive—in return for a baby whose arrival right now was, to say the least, inconvenient.

She almost surely had not talked with any of the other missing women. It was highly unlikely she knew any members of the ring. Had she, then, met one of the women who'd bought a baby? Met her and followed the trail back, hoping to get in on some of the money her new friend talked about spending?

That didn't seem likely, but then neither did any other idea I'd come up with so far.

Of course if she'd *had* any such information, it was probably in her purse. And her purse, if it still existed at all, was probably in that unknown place where she'd been held. But I had to look. And look I did.

I don't say it was totally impossible something small could have slipped past me, something deliberately hidden, because I didn't want to tear the house apart the way I would if I were looking for drugs. And I put things back in the places I found them, as close as I could remember, because I didn't want Clara Hammond to have to clean behind me. So it wasn't as thorough a search as I would have made under other circumstances.

But on the other hand, Grace wasn't hiding contraband. Grace didn't have any reason to be hiding *anything*. She had no reason to expect anybody would be looking for anything. So I didn't think there was anything there that could have related to her murder that I didn't find.

And what I found was exactly nothing. A great big zero.

At this point I had a choice. I could go back to Fort Worth and make a whole lot of long-distance telephone calls back to Sherman. Or I could go and check into a motel and run up a local telephone bill. Or I could go to the Sherman Police Station and try to work my case in the midst of all their work. They wouldn't have minded that, of course, but I might have minded.

Or I could do exactly what I did do, which was to sit down in the living room—if that's what you want to call it—of Clara Hammond's house and begin to look through Grace's love letters and Grace's address book and Grace's calendar.

When I got through, I knew the names and addresses of all Grace's friends and I knew that 90 percent of them either weren't home or weren't answering their telephones. Most likely they were at work.

There was one name I recognized—was rather surprised to recognize—but it was one that would wait till I got back to Fort Worth.

From letters and calendars I knew when all Grace's doctor's appointments had been, and I knew a lot about what Grace and Tim Richards did in bed. But I still didn't know the first thing about what had happened to get Grace from this house to the ditch in the northeast corner of Fort Worth.

"Miss Hammond," I asked, "do you know whether Grace knew anybody who had a small baby?"

Miss Hammond cackled. "Miz Ralston," she said, "Grace worked in a day-care center. Grace worked in the *baby* room of a day-care center. You could just about say that outside of the people she went to school with, Grace didn't know anybody who didn't have a small baby."

I got the name of the day-care center—Lambie Pie, which I thought was just too cute for words—and I got its address and headed that way, stopping halfway there to get a Coke and a package of potato chips to calm my stomach. I have got to find time to go to the doctor, I told myself.

The director, owner, what-have-you wasn't at all happy about giving me the names of the women who used the day-care center. But we discussed the matter at some length, and she finally did admit, cautiously, that really there were only two babies under six months old, if that was what I wanted, and she guessed she could let me have those names.

I went to look at the babies. I always like to look at babies, even if it is in my professional capacity.

One of the babies was black; she couldn't have anything to do with this case, because every one of the kidnapped women was white, but I stopped to talk to her anyway. She cooed cheerfully and went on admiring her hands, which she'd clearly just discovered.

The other baby was white. He was a little doll, blue-eyed and auburn-haired, just three months old. His name was Christopher Talliaferro, pronounced "Tolliver," and Mrs. Lamb told me his mother should be on in just a few minutes, if I wanted to wait, and she was a real nice lady, she sure wouldn't mind talking to me, but the fact was, Grace hadn't taken care of Chris but just a few days because she'd quit just a week or two after Miz Tolliver started bringing him to the nursery, and . . .

I said I'd go wait in my car; I wouldn't dream of getting in her way while she was getting the babies ready for their parents.

She told me I couldn't miss Miz Tolliver; she drove a bright red Camaro.

I waited, and about fifteen minutes later Mrs.—or Miss—or Miz—or whatever—Talliaferro drove up in her bright red Camaro. She got out of the car in a neat dress-for-success suit I wouldn't think you'd need in the wilds of Sherman, Texas, and depressingly, I saw that she had auburn hair and blue eyes. Adoptive babies—especially black market ones—don't tend to be that closely matched to parents.

I got out of my car. "Mrs. Talliaferro?"

She turned. "Yes? Who are you? Do I know you?"

But it was curiosity, not fear. I produced my identification and said, "I'm Detective Ralston, Fort Worth Police Department. I'm investigating the murder of a woman who used to work here, and I'm trying to talk with everyone who knew her at all. Have you a minute right now?"

"Well, yes, I guess so. Murder? Who got murdered?" She was facing me, and I was seeing lively curiosity, not fear. No fear at all. If she'd just bought a black market baby, she ought to be afraid to talk to the police.

"Grace Hammond. She used to—"

"Oh, yes, the one used to work in the baby room. She was getting so big, bless her heart; I know exactly how she felt. I was just a *blimp* before Chris came. How can I help you? Murdered? She was *murdered*? Oh, my gosh, that wasn't her, that one that was found in the ditch, was that *Grace*? That's *awful*! Oh, my goodness, wait till I tell Rory, he'll have *cats*!" She put her hand over her mouth. "I'm sorry. I talk all the time. What did you want to know?"

I didn't, by now, want to know anything at all; she'd answered every possible question. But I thought for a minute and then asked lamely, "Have you seen her since she left the nursery?"

"Oh, no, if I had, I would have been sure to say hi, she was so nice to Chris and—"

"Did she mention anything to you last time you saw her about having any plans to go to Fort Worth?"

"Oh, no, she just handed Chris back to me with his clothes change and—"

"Thank you, Mrs. Talliaferro, that's all I needed to know."

I left. Fast. Before she could start on another nonstop talkathon.

Whenever I'm in Sherman, I try to make time to get ice cream at Ashburn's. That's Sherman's very own ice cream parlor, and they make some of the best ice cream I've ever had. I headed that way now, figuring I'd do some more thinking while I was waiting; I couldn't figure out why I was so hungry, but an ice cream should hold me until I got back to Fort Worth.

I sat down with my ice cream and looked at my watch. No wonder I was so hungry; it was six-thirty and I'd never bothered to have lunch. In fact, I'd sort of forgotten to have lunch, and furthermore I'd never had that planned talk with Chief Ellis.

Thinking something on the general order of "The hell with it," I called Harry and asked him if he could manage without me for one night. He asked me sadly if I thought he was an utter moron, and told me he'd take Becky and Hal out to a cafeteria for supper and give Hal extra money so he could eat breakfast at school. That is nothing new. Hal eats breakfast at school at least half the time.

I called Captain Millner, finding him—as I'd expected—still at the police station waiting not very patiently for my report. I told him I was spending the night in Sherman. He told me to be sure to save the receipts and asked me if I was onto something. "I don't think so," I told him.

"Then why are you spending the night in Sherman?"

"Because I'm not through here yet."

He said he guessed that was okay.

I called the Sherman Police Station. Chief Ellis was not there but had left a message for me; I was to go on over to his house if I wasn't headed back to Fort Worth.

Somehow I had a hunch he was going to invite me to spend the night there, quite chastely of course, with him and his wife. I didn't want to do that—I am uncomfortable in houses I don't know—so before I went there, I very carefully went and got a room at the Holiday Inn. I could not escape being invited for supper, but that was all right; Mrs. Ellis was a bright, cheerful woman, tall and thin but a good cook withal, who was well up on her husband's cases.

I told him I was probably covering ground his people had already covered, and he said that was okay. Then he added, "Actually I don't think you are. Thing is, we don't have any idea why she went missing. And you do."

I didn't tell him I didn't really at all. I didn't tell him I was at this moment doing no more than playing a hunch. But hunch or not, it looked better all the time.

After supper I managed to excuse myself and return to the Holiday Inn, to sit down with Grace's telephone book and resume calling the people Grace had known.

This time I got answers at most of the phones. I had figured out what I was going to say: I was investigating Grace's death—we thought it was probably some crazy mass murderer, but we had to look at everything—there was a possibility of suicide—was she depressed about the baby—do you know how she'd reacted around other people's babies—do you have a baby yourself? That was the first thing I really wanted to know.

Most of the people I talked with didn't have babies. The two who did I had more questions for: Did Grace seem upset about the idea of childbirth? Did Grace come visit you in the hospital?

Grace, it seemed, was an avid hospital visitor. And yes, she'd visited her friends in the hospital. Which told me her friends had been in the hospital, which was the second of the things I really wanted to know.

There were four names in the telephone book who apparently were no longer in Sherman. Claudia Reynolds, Carolyn Sullivan, Jackie Patten, and Sue Hudson. There were referrals on Claudia and Sue's telephones; Claudia had moved to Denton, Sue to Fort Worth. Throwing caution and the thought of the telephone bill to the winds—the bill would go on my Visa card along with the rest of the motel bill, but ultimately the city of Fort Worth was going to pay it—I called them and went through the same spiel.

Claudia did not have a baby. Sue said, "What do you mean 'baby,' I'm not even married yet." Then she giggled. "Oh, well, I know it isn't considered necessary anymore, but when I was a kid, I used to ask my mother if you could have a baby without being married and she said yes, but it isn't polite. Well, call me polite, okay? Sorry I can't help you, Mrs. Ralston."

The message on the other two numbers was less informative; it amounted to little more than "We are sorry but the number you are calling has been disconnected."

That was all I could do on those, I guessed, so I'd wait till morning and get Ellis to work with me—we'd go talk to neighbors and see what we could find out about where the people had gone.

And then I picked up a newspaper I'd bought on the way back to my room, opened a Coke, and settled down to read. I froze at the headline story:

"Textbook Suicide" Ruled Homicide

Houston (AP)—Two police detectives worked more than five years to convince authorities that a Louisiana woman didn't kill herself, but was unknowingly fed an overdose of barbituates by three people who wanted to sell her baby.

I read on through the story, mentally congratulating the two Houston detectives for their determined acumen and their stubbornness, and then I leaned back and put the paper down. No, this didn't of course have anything to do with my case. This was a Houston case, and the suspects seemed to be working originally out of New Orleans. But it told me I was right—as Harry had agreed I had to be—that anything people will pay that much for, somebody else will supply if he has to kill to get it.

My theory was looking better and better. No, I couldn't say that. It was lousy; the thought of people like that in the world was a thoroughly depressing one. But the theory was looking more and more convincing.

I went to sleep and dreamed about dead women trying even in death to defend their babies . . .

I didn't sleep well at all. But then I never do in a strange bed.

□ 8 □

Ellis agreed with me that we'd better find out where Carolyn Sullivan and Jackie Patten had gone. It occurred to me belatedly that if a woman who had not been pregnant suddenly showed up with a baby, her friends would ask a lot of questions which might be hard to answer if she didn't have adoption papers to show them. It would be simpler to move away and then show up later with a laughing insistence, "Oh, you just couldn't tell—I never did get very big."

Although if a crooked lawyer or two was in on the scheme, adoption papers might not be that hard to come by.

Fortunately Grace's address book listed addresses as well as telephone numbers. Carolyn Sullivan lived on Crockett Street; we decided to go there first for no particular reason except that it was closer. It was also, we found out, easier: Carolyn Sullivan had been living with her parents—or sort of with her parents. They had turned the attic into a little apartment for her, and she'd had her own telephone line run up there. Her mother was at home. Carolyn had moved to Denison. No, Carolyn wasn't married and she didn't have any children and Mrs. Sullivan couldn't imagine why we were asking. And no, Carolyn and Grace hadn't been particularly close friends anyway, it was just that they had been in the same graduating class in high school—before Grace dropped out of school—and Carolyn had been class secretary and Grace had probably needed to call her about . . .

We went on to try to find Jackie Patten.

It was a small frame house with a front porch and a fenced backyard. There was a persimmon tree in the front, its fruit looking innocently inviting. I laughed. "I bit one of those in September once," I said, "and I couldn't talk for two hours."

Ellis grinned, looking up into the tree. "I know what you mean. They're sure not fit to eat till after the first frost."

"Or any other time, as far as I'm concerned anymore," I said. We glanced into the backyard, at the doghouse, barbecue grill, and picnic table. Funny the Pattens hadn't taken those when they moved, unless they were things that belonged with the house. But they certainly hadn't taken them, and they certainly had gone—the front yard was grown up in weeds, and there was a FOR RENT sign nailed to the porch post—without a telephone number to call.

We went to the house on the right and found nobody at home.

In the house on the left was an old man who was, he told us, retired from the railroad. He was still wearing railroad boots, and a watch chain was stretched across a chubby midsection. His ruddy face beamed, his blue eyes sparkled, and his sparse white hair blew in the breeze created by an electric fan. Yes, he told us, he knew the Pattens—Jackie and Nick. They'd lived there a couple of years, he said, with a big dog they called Roger, only Roger died last winter and he guessed that was why they'd left the doghouse. Yes, they'd adopted a baby 'long about March or April, he guessed; anyways it was in the spring.

No, he didn't know where they'd moved to; he'd probably get a card from them come Christmas, but other than that . . .

Well, the house, that was owned by Polly Kittles. No, he didn't know her address. No, he didn't know her phone number. She went to the Baptist church and she used to be a friend of his wife, rest her soul, and he knew her by sight, but that was all he knew.

And he hoped the Pattens weren't in no trouble, quiet people they were, they kept themselves to themselves as the saying goes, but poor Miz Patten, she was so unhappy, she'd had them three misses, you know, everybody in the neighborhood knew that, and she'd been in the hospital so much, and . . .

Ellis and I looked at each other, and I told the retired brakeman that no, the Pattens weren't in any trouble. We just needed to talk with them, that was all.

We went to a 7-Eleven and looked for Kittles in the telephone book. The only one we found was George Kittles; Ellis said he thought that might be the right one, and we called it. Polly Kittles was home and said she'd be glad to talk to us.

Polly Kittles lived in a house not very much different from the one she'd rented to the Pattens. It had electric blue carpet, a tattered brown sofa, and a couple of recliner chairs of indeterminate color, indeterminate because of the crocheted throws that completely covered them. She had jammed a small kitchen table against the front window of the living room, with part of a room air conditioner sitting on the table which otherwise was piled with magazines, letters, bills, and several months' worth of mail. Two large black cats wandered around the living room; they were almost twice the size of my cat, and I asked her what kind they were. "Oh, they're just cats," she said, stroking one of them.

It did not purr; it also did not mew. It just strolled casually away, followed closely by the other.

"Now what can I do for you?" she asked, following it by the inevitable comment, "You sure don't look much like a cop."

I couldn't resist any longer. "What," I asked, "does a cop look like?"

"Oh, *you* know," she said vaguely, fortunately not taking offense. "You wanted to know about the Pattens, you said?"

"That's right, Miz Kittles," Ellis answered. "You know, they used to know Mary Grace Hammond, and we're trying to talk to all her friends—you did know Mary Grace went off to Fort Worth and got herself kilt, didn't you?"

That set her off; it was two or three minutes before Ellis was able to steer her back to the Pattens. I kept quiet. There's a lot of difference between Fort Worth and the little towns north and east of it, and I expected Ellis knew his people a lot better than I did. Besides, as overtired as I was, if I didn't watch out, I'd be making somebody mad, and that's a real good way to lose a cooperative witness.

It really didn't do any good. What it boiled down to was, Mrs. Kittles didn't know where the Pattens went. She'd been sorry to lose them; they were good tenants and she hadn't rented the house since. They'd told her Nick got a real good job offer and they were moving real sudden, they didn't have a new address yet and they'd let her know just as soon as they got one—well, no, he hadn't mentioned what town, but—well, no, they hadn't sent the new address . . .

Deposit? Yes, she owed them seventy-five-dollars' deposit, and she'd reminded them of that herself, and Nick'd said, "Give it to the Red Cross."

Yes, of *course* she did it. And she'd kept the receipt, so she could send it to them when they sent the new address. And no, she'd already *said* she didn't know what town . . .

Work? Well, he'd been working at the meat-packing plant ever since he got out of the Army, but of course he'd left that.

We called the packing plant.

He'd not only left, he'd left with no notice, and yes, if the police wanted to talk with the personnel department, they'd be glad to cooperate.

We met with a Dorothy Gordon in personnel, who properly asked to see our identification before producing a manila folder with a blue-trimmed label on it. "PATTEN, Nicholas T." was typed on the label.

"As I told you over the telephone," said Dorothy Gordon, who hadn't informed me I didn't look like a cop, "Mr. Patten did leave us with virtually no notice. He told his supervisor that he'd had a much better job offer in Arlington and would be leaving immediately; he apologized for leaving so suddenly, but he said that one of the conditions of the offer was that he start immediately."

"Do you have any forwarding address, Ms. Gordon?" I asked.

"It's Mrs., but please, just Dorothy. No, he didn't give us one. He said he didn't have an address yet and he would write when he did. He would have had a check coming, of course, and in fact . . . Yes. It was mailed to his old address and it came back stamped MOVED, NO FORWARDING ADDRESS. This is really quite inexplicable, you know; he'd been with us five years, and he's a very dependable worker; in fact, let's see, no, he never took one sick day the entire time."

"When did he leave, Dorothy?" I asked.

"Hmm, let's see . . . September . . . yes, it was September third."

September 3. The same day Grace left. That might have been coincidence, or it might have been—something other than coincidence. And of course they might not have gone to Arlington at all. That might very well have just been a smoke screen for the benefit of an inquisitive boss.

I asked whether the company had a credit union and was told that it did.

We got other things that might help—names and addresses of relatives mainly—and left.

"The credit union won't tell us shit," Ellis said, and I agreed. But by now I hoped I had enough for a court order to get the records opened to us.

The judge said I didn't.

So there was no way of knowing whether the Pattens had had a savings account, and if so, whether it showed any large amounts taken out lately. There was no way of knowing . . .

We went over to the credit union to see whether the people there would tell us anything. Without telling any lies, Ellis carefully and neatly gave the impression the Pattens had been reported as missing, and the credit union official we talked with unbent enough to tell us, cautiously, that she was sure the Pattens were all right, as they had written several checks recently in Arlington.

Arlington. Okay, that was a start. Maybe they really had moved to Arlington.

I'd done about all I could do in Sherman. I left Ellis at his office, stopped by McDonald's for a hamburger, and headed for home, thinking of that one name I recognized from Grace's address book. Dr. Frank Kirk. Who ran an abortion clinic in Fort Worth, Texas. I wanted, badly, to have another talk with Dr. Frank Kirk.

I found three patrolmen I'd never seen before sitting in the major case squad office morosely fiddling with newly installed computer terminals. There had been, I was told, 17,672 reported births in Tarrant County last year. There were no fewer than thirty different reporting agencies involved. But 13,552 of those came from areas which kept their own computer tapes, and all our computer people had to do was to enter the tapes into a program Roddy had set up. That left only about 6000 to be entered manually. Which wasn't quite as bad as we had anticipated.

All the same, my borrowed patrolmen didn't seem to love me very much.

Squeezing past the patrolmen to my nearly inaccessible desk, I looked for messages. De Ridder, Louisiana, said Grace Carstairs was home and in good health, and did I need to talk with her?

By now I'd almost forgotten asking about Grace Carstairs.

Mrs. Murray appreciated my help and was quite put out at her daughter's lack of consideration.

That was nice of Mrs. Murray.

Frank Kirk wanted me to call him at 8:01 A.M.

Frank Kirk wanted me to call him at 9:20 A.M.

Frank Kirk wanted me to call him at 1:26 P.M.

That was interesting, I thought, and called Frank Kirk at the number he'd left, which turned out to be the small private hospital near his clinic. Frank Kirk was in surgery, the receptionist said. I asked her to leave word that I'd drop by the hospital about four-twenty to meet with him.

"So what did he want?" Captain Millner asked. He'd walked in, unnoticed, while I was on the phone.

I shrugged. "I'll let you know when I know."

Millner looked over at the patrolmen. "What's the purpose of all that?" he asked, more resignedly than curiously.

I told him it was a fishing expedition, and he nodded. It is a fact that detectives sometimes go on fishing expeditions, and usually they do not know what they're fishing for until they see what surfaces.

The tapes had been entered while I was in Sherman, I was told, and maybe a fourth of the manual entries were already in. I called Roddy and asked him if he could sort what was already entered, and he said he could if I wanted to come pick up the printouts. I didn't exactly want to walk all over Fort Worth carrying a sheaf of printouts, considering their size, but on the other hand, I did want the information. I told Roddy I would come get the printouts.

And, not exactly to my surprise, I hit paydirt almost immediately, while I was looking at the names of parents.

Jackie Patten, who everybody we talked to had assured us had never completed a pregnancy—who, we had been told, had finally given up and adopted a baby last March—had, according to Tarrant County vital statistics, given birth to a baby.

Jacqueline Marie Patten and Nicholas Timothy Patten had, on March 7, become the parents of an eight-pound two-ounce baby boy. The baby was delivered by a midwife named Rachel Strada.

Arlington—they had apparently moved to Arlington. Probably we could trace them through utility records, unless they had moved to an apartment with utilities paid.

But I wasn't going to get very far checking with utilities now; it was after four o'clock, and Captain Millner was wandering through the halls shouting, "Day watch, clear out!"

□ □ □

We were sitting in the doctors' lounge. Kirk had a cup of coffee, and I was drinking a Coke. "It was the name," he told me. "When it turned up in the newspaper this morning I remembered it. Back in—oh, sometime in the spring, maybe March, April, a Mary Grace Hammond called me for an appointment. She didn't cancel and she didn't show up. Called again a week later with the same results, and then did it again a week after *that*. She called once more; Hazel asked me if I wanted to make the appointment or not, and I told her sure, I'd see the girl if she showed up. And that time she did."

"And?"

"Well—I treat patients, not just pelvises, if you know what I mean."

I nodded. I knew exactly what he meant. Any woman who has had very much experience being treated by military doctors knows exactly what he means.

"I took her into my office," he went on, "and sat down with her. Okay, to start with, I could guess by looking at her that she was four and a half, five months, and I don't care what the law says, by five months you've got a potentially viable fetus, and that's too damn late to go to thinking about an abortion. I've fought too hard to *save* five-month fetuses. Did, a few times. Not often. But—anyhow, on top of that, she was a kid, acted younger even than her age called for. And she was—ambivalent. She didn't know what she wanted. She wanted an abortion but she didn't want an abortion but she didn't want to have the baby but she did want to have the baby but she didn't know how to raise it. I told her she didn't need me; she needed a psychologist or a psychiatrist who'd help her sort out her feelings, and I offered to give her a name of somebody who wouldn't charge much. I told her—from the way she was talking, the way she was acting, she'd not be able to handle the emotional trauma if she did find somebody who'd do an abortion, and don't let anybody kid you, there is emotional trauma.

And so she left and never came back. That's the last I heard from her."

"And that's what you wanted to tell me?"

"Not all of it. She—asked me if I could find somebody to buy her baby. I told her that was illegal; I told her I could maybe get a lawyer in on it and we could find somebody who'd pay her medical bills in return for adopting, but that was all anybody could do. And she told me one of her friends had bought a baby for ten thousand dollars—said she'd saved for years and years to do it—and she, Grace, I mean, said ten thousand dollars would really help her a lot. I tried to talk some sense into her. When that didn't work, I asked her if she knew where her friend had bought the baby, and she told me she couldn't remember but she'd write me if she found out."

"And did she?"

He shook his head. "I never heard from her again. I did wonder, a time or two. But then all that stuff hit the paper about the Mexican babies that were being sold, and I figured that was what she was talking about and I just—well, I guess I just forgot about it until right now."

Talking half to myself, I said, "Well, I guessed it. Most, if not all, of the others were kidnapped, but Grace—the poor little girl—walked in on purpose."

"Ignorance can be cured," Kirk said. "Stupidity can't. I'm sorry, I need to go check on a patient."

"If you hear anything else—"

"I'll call you. Yeah. But I don't expect to."

I went on home and prepared meatloaf and green beans and baked potatoes and salad for my loving family, and I went to bed very early, thinking that after I got off work Thursday—tomorrow; I had nearly lost track of days—I was going to have to go to the grocery store if I could make my stomach behave itself long enough.

That reminded me of something else. I crawled out of bed

and stuck the Tagamet bottle in my purse so that I'd remember to call the pharmacy about getting it refilled.

Thursday morning I called Arlington, getting a detective named Kathy Stein, who assured me there was no need for me to drive over; she'd try to find the Pattens for me. That helped; I could now go and look for Rachel Strada.

That was when I ran into another blank wall.

Rachel Strada wasn't in the telephone book—I checked Fort Worth, Arlington, Hurst, the mid-cities—you name it, I checked it, and Rachel Strada wasn't in any of them. I called 817 directory assistance and 214 directory assistance, and nobody had a Rachel Strada.

I swore—mildly—and grabbed the telephone book again, to call the Tarrant County Medical Society.

That was where I met yet another blank wall. The secretary sadly informed me the Tarrant County Medical Society had no information at all on midwives. None. Not any.

Reluctantly she did part with the telephone number of the Texas Board of Medical Examiners in Austin. Maybe they could help me, she said not very helpfully.

I called the Texas Board of Medical Examiners in Austin. The secretary I talked with said she didn't know very much about midwives because they don't go through that licensing board, but she did know they aren't exactly licensed, not exactly, and maybe I had better speak to the attorney, Mr. Martinez. She transferred me.

Mr. Martinez told me that midwives aren't exactly licensed, but they do get certificates. They go through the Health Department (the Texas State Health Department, not the county one, he explained in answer to my question), where they have to take an exam, and after they pass the exam, they're given a certificate saying they successfully passed the exam.

"Do they have to retake it annually or anything like that?" I asked.

"Well, I don't know about that," Mr. Martinez told me, and referred me to *Vernon's Texas Statutes* 45121. Civil Statutes, that was, he added.

I did not go and look up *Vernon's Texas Statutes*. It would not tell me what I needed to know, which was, what, if any, agency—state, federal, or local—would have a file on the locations of the midwives.

Mr. Martinez did add one interesting fact. He said Texas had many lay midwives—not trained medical people—and as long as they passed the exam and did not try to practice medicine, nobody worried too much about what they did.

I had always thought delivering babies was practicing medicine. Apparently, at least at present, the state of Texas does not agree with me.

I telephoned the Texas State Department of Health. The secretary said oh, I really needed to talk with Mrs. Dubs, and she would transfer me. She transferred me. Mrs. Dubs's secretary said I really needed to talk with Miss Jones.

Stonewalled again. Miss Jones was out of the office for the day and her secretary was sick and nobody else could possibly help me, sorry but that was the way it was, and they would have somebody call me tomorrow. Definitely tomorrow for sure.

I said, "The hell with it," and told Gary Hollister, who as I have said is at least nominally my boss, that I was going to take a half a day off. I said I thought I deserved it. Gary said that was a relief, because he was going to be in trouble if he had to turn in all that overtime on me.

I headed for Town and Country Pharmacy, where the pharmacist sweetly informed me that he couldn't possibly refill the Tagamet prescription. "Why not?" I demanded. "It says right here on the label, three refills."

"Mrs. Ralston," he said, "you got that prescription in 1981 and you haven't refilled it since. Just because you had a stomach ulcer in 1981 doesn't mean you have a stomach ulcer now."

"But—"

"I'll tell you what. I'll call your doctor, and if *he* wants me to refill it, then I will, okay? But it'll take a little while."

Confident that the doctor would approve the refill, I lounged around the front of the drugstore, stealthily reading *Mad* magazine and beginning a paperback romance, and finally the pharmacist came out and said, "Mrs. Ralston, I'm sorry, but your doctor says he can't okay a refill without seeing you first."

I thought, but did not say, rude words. I bought the paperback romance, a bag of peanut M & M's, and a new antacid that said it was designed especially for women, and then I got back in my car and drove home, where I gobbled antacids. Last time I had an ulcer I didn't know it until I innocently took an aspirin—aspirins are not recommended for ulcer patients—and the next thing I knew the EMTs were hauling me off to the hospital insisting I was having a heart attack.

I *told* them it was my stomach, but they didn't believe me.

Anyhow the antacids helped, and I flopped down on the bed to read the romance, only I wound up going to sleep until Hal woke me up coming home. I commandeered him to go with me to the grocery store. I wanted to go to Sack and Save, and when I go there, I use Hal as an ex officio bag boy. He sits in the backseat and sings out the window while I'm driving.

I came off Denton Highway about dark, having done some other shopping as well, and swung up the loop to the Beach Street exit. We were almost to the place where Beach Street narrows for the bridge over Fossil Creek when suddenly—out of nowhere it seemed—a girl dashed across the road toward my car. I couldn't make out her face—she had on a lace scarf and her hair was over her eyes and she had on too much makeup; I guessed she was trying to look like Madonna—but she was waving her arms and shouting, and of course I hastily lowered the window to hear what she was saying.

"Your hood is about to fly open!" she shouted. "It looks like there's something wrong with it—you need to get out of the car and check . . ."

I glanced toward the hood. It looked all right to me, but of course the night was getting dark and she might be able to see something I couldn't. She grabbed the door handle and began to open the door, urging me again to get out and check—I had to get out of the car . . .

She was too eager to get me out of the car. Much too eager.

I snatched the door and jerked it closed and snapped the lock, reaching back to lock Hal's door before she had time to reach for it.

The pretty face I still couldn't quite make out under the overdose of—yes, *smeared* makeup, deliberately smeared—twisted, as she tried to reach inside the car to get at the lock. I began to roll up the window, moving my foot from the brake to the gas as I did so, and out of the corner of my eye I saw the hooded man come up out of the ditch on the right side with a long piece of pipe in his hand—no, it wasn't a pipe— "Get down, Hal!" I shouted.

"What?" He was confused; he hadn't figured out yet what was going on. But then why should he figure it out? He wasn't quite sixteen years old. In his world people don't try to kill people. Not yet.

"Get down *now!*" I tried to steer directly toward the man, accelerating—I had to stop him but I didn't stop him; I had to stop him, but fireworks aren't legal in Fort Worth and no firecracker ever was so loud as the one that shattered my windshield—and I couldn't tell where the car was going because it didn't seem to be going where I told it to go . . .

"Hal, are you all right?" I shouted.

I couldn't tell whether he was hurt or not. He was crying or shouting, I couldn't tell which and I couldn't stop to check, because the man with the shotgun was still out there somewhere. I was driving blind, steering with my left hand while my right hand dug the pistol out of the side pocket of my purse, but the car was still fishtailing; I'd gone off the road a time or two and the shoulder isn't lined up even with the road, so every time I got back up on the road I started fishtailing again. Luckily I had shatterproof glass, so that instead of having a car full of glass splinters we had a car full of little roughly rectangular chunks of glass, but all the same I was still blinking glass out of my face and steering blind, steering with my left hand while my right hand raised the pistol into firing position if I could see anybody to fire at only I couldn't . . .

And I slammed into a small tree, too small for me to see it as fast as I was trying to see, but then of course I couldn't make the car move at all—I had hit a tree and somewhere out there a man with a shotgun was hunting me like Harry hunts deer and my son was in the backseat . . .

Sobbing blindly, I returned fire and then dropped the pistol on the seat long enough to shift into reverse and back away from the tree, to straighten the car and drive slowly, controlled, back onto Beach Street, trying to see through the wreckage of the windshield that hadn't all fallen away from the frame.

I heard the shotgun go off a second time, but I couldn't tell where it hit. It didn't hit the windshield this time, maybe because I didn't have very much windshield left, but it hit the car somewhere. I knew because I felt the car jerk, and I heard Hal shouting, "Mom! Mom!"

I fired back twice more, and I think I hit somebody somewhere, because I heard somebody outside the car yelp. Then the man and the girl were running toward a car I didn't have time to get a good look at, and they were scrambling into it and they were leaving.

I think I tried to go after them.

I think I tried to start the car and head down Beach Street after them.

I couldn't see their license plate—they had covered it with mud, probably deliberately, and I never had a chance to see what kind of car it was except that it was light-colored and small and probably not very old. A hatchback. A compact or subcompact. Like maybe a third of the cars on the road nowadays.

I tried to start the car and head down Beach Street after

them, but my car didn't seem to want to go very far, and then it stopped and I couldn't make it start, and I saw their tail lights vanish as they turned left onto Saginaw-Watauga Road. I could just make that out.

And then I got my car door open and staggered out of the car and tried to open Hal's door and couldn't and then remembered I'd locked it, and I started to reach in to unlock it, only by that time he'd gotten it open himself and had stumbled out of the car saying something like "Mommy," which I don't think he's said in the last four or five years.

"Are you okay, Hal? Are you okay?"

I guess he said he was okay or else I figured out that he was okay, and by then another car had stopped to see what had happened. I recognized them vaguely; they were neighbors up the street; and I asked them to take Hal and me to Stop and Go.

I called Harry from Stop and Go. That is, I tried to call Harry, but Becky reminded me this was Thursday and he had of course gone to help with bingo. I told her to call the lodge and tell him I was at Stop and Go and I had had a sort of an accident and yes, we were all right, but I needed Harry . . .

And then I called the police emergency number, and pretty soon Captain Millner was there, and several patrol cars and a crime scene unit and a wrecker.

Harry arrived relatively fast, considering he'd had to come from clear over by White Settlement Road.

The second shotgun round had hit the radiator. That was why I couldn't make the car go very far. The water had all fallen out, and my engine automatically cut off when it got too hot.

Stupidly I said, "But I just put the antifreeze in."

Harry said, "You need more than antifreeze now. Baby, you're in shock."

One of the carloads of people that had stopped to gawk included several of Hal's school friends, one being the ubiquitous Sammy, and I heard Hal saying importantly, "You should have seen it! It was a great big shotgun! A ten-gauge or something like that . . . Naah, I wasn't scared, was I, Mom?"

Then I could laugh—for a while.

Until I remembered Hal was the only Korean kid in Keller High School. On his school bus route. In Summerfields. Which made him quite easy to identify, if anybody wanted to attack me by attacking my children.

□9□

I WOULD NOT EXACTLY say that I slept well Thursday night. Or for that matter that I slept at all. I worried. And I worried. And I worried. And I flipped and flopped and rolled up in the covers and unrolled them and threw them on the floor and got up and put them back on the bed and worried some more.

I could hear Harry in the living room talking to somebody in Tierra del Fuego. He hadn't even tried to go to sleep.

The problem was that being shot at, although it is certainly no fun, is at least not totally unexpected on the job. But my family was not supposed to be involved. Nobody was supposed to shoot at me while I was off duty; nobody was supposed to shoot at my children.

We couldn't pull Hal out of school, and I clearly couldn't stay there with him, but how was I supposed to work with him that vulnerable? All I wanted to do was worry.

After some frantic telephoning we had worked it out that Harry, who could be late to work with few questions raised, would take him to school and see him safely into the building. The principal and other school personnel knew the situation now—we'd called them—and if any unfamiliar adult showed up, the Keller Police Department, which also had been advised of the situation, would be called at once. Sammy's parents, who live on an isolated dairy farm, would pick Hal and Sammy up, and the boys would go out and roam around with the cows and the milkers until Harry or I picked him up again. No stranger could get within a mile of the milking shed, which stands on an isolated knoll, without being spotted at once.

The next worry was Becky. Of course she is not as conspicuous as Hal—she is half Comanche and could easily pass for a tall Mexican. Comanches and Mexicans—especially Mexicans—are perfectly common in Fort Worth. She would be driving her own car, and the company she works for has a fenced parking lot you have to pass a guard to enter. But just in case they—whoever "they" might happen to be—had spotted her car, I talked her into going a roundabout way to work. Beach Street to Saginaw-Watauga Road—I mean Great Western Parkway; someday I'll get used to that—and then *left* on the alleged parkway, over to Denton Highway and across to Belknap, rather than the more direct right turn onto 35 and thence to the loop. Going that way, there won't be any isolated stretches of road where she could be ambushed, I told Harry, and he said, "Deb, I think you're worrying too much."

"What are you talking about?" I demanded. "After what happened—"

"Deb, they were after you. I don't think it was anything more than coincidence that Hal happened to be in the car." He bit his fingernail, staring at me and looking for a moment much older than his actual forty-six years, and said, "I would ask you to quit the job. But you wouldn't, so why bother? Just take it easy. You're figuring out precautions for the kids. Now how about figuring out some for yourself? And damn it, go to the *doctor*!" he yelled after me as I suddenly dashed in the direction of the bathroom with my hand over my mouth. "You were in the hospital for a week last time . . ." I didn't hear the rest.

"I'll go to the doctor when I get time," I told him three minutes later with as much dignity as I could muster. "I just forgot to take my antacids. And I'm being very careful. You don't need to worry about me."

One of the precautions I'd figured out—or rather, Captain Millner had ordered—was sitting on the kitchen counter. It was a single recharging unit for a walkie-talkie, not unlike the banks of chargers in the police station. From now on, until this was cleared up, I'd have not only a revolver but also a radio with me at all times. There would be no more of being unable to call for help when I was under fire.

I didn't want to put a shotgun in my personal car. Harry had one, of course, and for that matter I could get a department-issued one under the circumstances, but too many weapons are stolen out of cars. I didn't want to leave one in mine. But on the other hand, I also didn't want to be meandering down the streets of Fort Worth on the way to work clutching a shotgun to my bosom.

In the end, I'd just told Harry I'd be careful. I lay rigidly in bed thinking about being careful, and around 4 A.M. I finally dozed off for a restless and nightmare-filled couple of hours.

Friday morning I had to write a report. I found it surprisingly hard to do; I am not used to being the victim myself. Things were fuzzy in my memory. I guess the reason for that is that when I am at home, when I am jogging, when I am shopping, I am on my own time. I have shifted gears, I am in wife-and-mother mode, and things are not supposed to happen then that would not happen to any ordinary suburban housewife. And the result was that instead of reacting professionally at once, I almost went into shock. Of course memories were foggy.

I managed to sort them out and write the report anyway. I still hadn't gotten any telephone call from Arlington, and I didn't, I decided, have time to wait for one. When Stein called, somebody could take the message; I wanted to go out and check on some other things. I grabbed my notebook and was reaching for the keys to a detective car when the telephone rang. Dutch, who for some reason had talked the *Star-Telegram* into giving him (or lending him) the last six months' worth of letters to the editor (published and unpublished), reached over the bulky file on his desk and grabbed the phone. "Major case unit, Van Flagg—yeah, just a minute." He pushed the HOLD button and pointed at me.

"Ralston," I said, and a crisp voice said, "Stein, Arlington. About Patten."

I sat back down. "Yeah, Kathy, what've you got?"

"Well, September eighth they moved into an apartment complex east of the college. But right after they moved in, they got an Akita—that's a damn big dog, and it scared the hell out of some people and they were asked to move back out. So they got a little house west of the apartments. I haven't been over to try to talk to them yet—figured you'd kind of like to do that yourself."

"Did anybody mention them having a baby?" I didn't know why I asked that. By now we'd pretty well established the fact that they had possession of a baby.

"Yeah, about five months old, little boy. They call him Timmy. One set of neighbors said Jackie didn't seem to know how to take care of him, but you know, that's not all that unusual with a first baby. Especially if it's—well—not prepared for in the usual way." I'd told Kathy the background.

I said I'd be there in about half an hour or so, depending on what traffic looked like, and Kathy said she'd wait for me.

In the car I got to thinking about something I should have been thinking about already. Nick Patten, until a few weeks ago, had worked on the line at a meat-processing plant. Jackie Patten didn't have a job at all.

It was the Akita that triggered the thought, because one time we were thinking about getting one, until we found out a perfectly ordinary, not show-quality, Akita pup runs three hundred dollars or more. We already knew they'd shelled out ten thousand dollars for a baby—that had to have totally depleted their savings and every loan they could scrape up. So where had the Pattens gotten the money to buy an Akita, and where had Nick

Patten gotten the money to quit his job with no warning and move to Arlington?

I hadn't even thought about looking at newspapers in days, except the one I glanced at in Sherman, and I hadn't checked the bulletin board. I'd read what had crossed my desk and that was about it. So what *had* been going on? What was the rest of the department working? What were the departments in neighboring towns working? What was the FBI working? One of them, somewhere, was working on something that would tell me where the Pattens had come up with a lot of money.

All I could think of right now was bank robbery. There just aren't very many places that have that kind of money lying around for the taking.

Maybe I was unduly cynical. Maybe Nick really did get a good job.

I was too curious and wound up to wait until I got to Arlington. I pulled off the road and called the FBI, getting special agent Dub Arnold. Dub told me there hadn't been any bank robberies with that kind of take in the area in months. "What are you trying to stir up, Deb?" he asked me.

I told him, and he said, "You know, I just have a hunch that when you get your case all straightened out, it's going to turn out to be my case too."

"I wouldn't be a bit surprised," I agreed. Of course interstate trafficking in black market babies is a federal offense.

"Well, I'll tell you what," he said. "You give me what you've got on Patten, and I'll see if my boss'll okay me just doing a little background check, all right?"

I gave him name, date of birth, place of birth, last known address, last known place of employment, Social Security number, and a rough physical description. He said, "It may take a few days."

"Take as long as you need, just so's I get the information tomorrow," I said, and he chuckled and hung up.

Most police officers think the FBI's reputation is somewhat overrated—the Bureau has sort of a habit of grabbing the glory on every joint operation, even when the joint operation is 90 percent local. But there are some things the FBI is undeniably very good at, and this sort of thing is among them. I was grateful to have the help. With any luck at all, Dub would track down in a matter of days information I'd never otherwise get at all.

I took the time, while I was at a phone anyway, to call the school. Yes, Hal was there. Yes, they were sure; he'd just taken a message for one of the teachers.

For no apparent reason my worry had let up slightly, and I found myself humming as I drove toward Arlington. By nine-thirty I was sitting in Kathy Stein's office. I'd never met her before, and I'd guess her to be about my age, maybe a little older. And a lot less likely, I thought ruefully, to be told she didn't look like a cop—Kathy was a black woman nearly six feet tall; from looking at her I would guess that in a fight she could easily whip most men.

She had an address for the Pattens, and we drove out there in my car. Of course as we had no warrants of any kind, Jackie could refuse to let us in the house, much less talk to us—well, we knew that. Probably Jackie didn't know it, but we were going to have to tell her. As she was a definite suspect, we were required to give her a Miranda warning before we talked with her.

So of course we stood on the front steps and gave her a Miranda warning, while an Akita strained at her hand on its collar. She put the dog inside the fence and returned to us, trying very hard to look puzzled. She didn't succeed very well. I'd guess her to be maybe twenty-eight, but she seemed younger; she had very fair, very freckled skin, a fluffy mass of orangy hair, and pale blue eyes. She wasn't as tall as Kathy, but she was a lot taller than me, and she moved with an awkward coltishness, as if she still weren't quite used to her size.

The house was a lot nicer than the one they'd had in Sherman, and most of the furniture looked new. I wondered again where the money had come from. And I wondered again whether she knew, or whether the desire for a baby had so fogged her that she refused to know.

She knew something was wrong, though, and the acting job wasn't very good. "Police?" she said. "What are you talking about? I haven't done anything wrong."

Whoever had told her to bat her eyelashes at the police hadn't stopped to think that she might get female police.

"Glad to hear it," Kathy said heartily. "In that case you won't mind a bit if we talk to you, right?" She leaned on the door frame, looking very big and very black.

"Well—"

"It's extremely important, Mrs. Patten," I said.

She looked gratefully at me. Kathy and I hadn't started out to play good-cop/bad-cop, but it seemed Jackie was dropping us into those roles. I have never in my life been able to be the bad cop in that game; as one man once told me, "*You're* a cop? But—but—but—you look like somebody's sweet little auntie!"

Kathy was somewhat less likely to look like somebody's sweet little auntie. Except, maybe, Grace Jones's.

We had gone on looking at Jackie Patten, neither of us saying anything else, and somewhere in the house a baby began to cry. She turned back from the door, a frantic look on her face, and said, "Yes, come in, come on in."

"May I see the baby?" I asked. "I just love babies; I have a brand-new grandson. Is yours a boy or a girl?"

"Boy," she said. "He's five months old." She looked tired as she turned toward the back of the house. Kathy, with a glance at me, stayed in the living room. "He's teething, and it really makes him miserable, and then I get so sorry for him I don't know what to do." She forced a laugh. "The pediatrician says babies can tell when you don't know what to do, and that makes them cry even more."

"That's true, of course," I agreed, following her into the bedroom she'd made into a nursery. A Jenny Lind crib, a dresser-changing table, lots of toys, a nice oak rocking chair for her to rock the baby—beautiful baby clothes and wall hangings and a

Busy Box he'd probably be playing with when he felt better, as well as a butterfly mobile he'd clearly been chewing on. I felt sorry for her, suddenly, as I hadn't before; but I felt a lot sorrier for the baby's real mother, who was probably dead, and for the baby's real father, who was going to have to raise the baby alone; and sorriest of all for the baby himself, who had already been deprived of one mother and was soon to lose another.

I leaned against the door and watched her change him. "Mrs. Patten," I said, abruptly abandoning my original plan of attack, "I know you love that baby, because I have three adopted children and I know how much I love them. The last thing in the world I'd want to do is make anything harder for you or for the baby. So I'm not going to play games with you. I'm going to tell you up front why we're here. Mrs. Patten, I adopted my children legally. You didn't. That's a black market baby. You bought him for money, and before very long we're going to be able to prove it. You'll make it a lot easier on yourself and the baby too if you tell the truth and give him up now."

"You're completely absurd," she said unconvincingly. I had seen her jump, and now she picked up a talcum powder can with shaky hands. "I can even show you his birth certificate. It *says* he's mine."

"You're not the first person to dream up that scheme—if you did dream it up, which I doubt; I expect somebody else dreamed it up for you. Yes, I know you have his birth certificate. How come none of your friends knew you were pregnant?"

She shrugged. "I just never did show very much."

She'd weigh, maybe, a hundred pounds. She'd be showing by the second month. "Where was he born?" I asked.

"In Fort Worth."

"Why in Fort Worth? I thought you still lived in Sherman when he was born. Where in Fort Worth?"

She wasn't expecting those questions, and she didn't have answers for them. "Oh—er—in—ah—at home. I mean where we were staying—uh—temporarily in Fort Worth. Just for a week. Nickie was job hunting."

"Where were you staying? Where in Fort Worth?"

She shrugged. "We stayed at a motel."

"So the baby was born in a motel?"

"That's right. It was—um—a LaQuinta."

"Which one?"

She shrugged again. "Umm—it's in Forth Worth. Kind of close to a mall. Northeast Mall I think they call it."

"That's in North Richland Hills. The motel, I mean, not the mall."

"Maybe it is. I don't know."

"There's no maybe to it," I told her. "That motel is in North Richland Hills."

"Okay, it's in North Richland Hills. So what?"

"So how come the birth was registered in the unincorporated area of Tarrant County?"

"Maybe they got mixed up?" She was asking, not telling.

"They don't get that kind of mixed up, Mrs. Patten," I told her. "Who delivered the baby?"

"A midwife. Her name was Rachel Strada." She said that fast, a memorized lesson.

"Okay, what does Rachel Strada look like?"

She shrugged, pushed her strawberry blond hair out of her eyes. "I don't remember. I think—I think I was all upset."

"Is Rachel Strada black or white?"

"I think she's white."

"You *think*?"

"I told you I was all upset."

"Where did you locate Rachel Strada?"

"My husband did that."

"How long were you in labor?"

"Oh—uh—uh—about three hours."

"That's funny, the average for a first baby is closer to eight to twelve hours."

"So I'm not average."

"How much did you pay for the baby, Jackie?"

"This is my baby and you get out of my house!" Clutching the screaming baby to her breast, she added, "Listen, this is *my* baby, but if I *had* bought him it would be okay, because any woman who is so crummy she'd sell her own baby for ten thousand dollars shouldn't have one!"

"I didn't mention a figure," I said softly. She stared at me, her mouth open, and I added, "But yes, I know it was ten thousand dollars. And before I go, there's something I want you to know. The mother didn't sell that baby. The baby was stolen from the mother, and the mother was probably murdered. A legal adoption is just that—legal. And usually fair. But black market adoptions are illegal because they're unfair, to the birth mother or the adoptive mother or the baby or all three. Think about that, Jackie, and call me when you've thought it over."

I headed down the hall, motioning to Kathy to follow me as I passed through the living room. Behind me I could hear Jackie Patten shrieking over the baby's wails, "You're lying, you're lying!" But there was fear in her voice, real fear and a lot of it.

In the car Kathy asked, "What do you think?"

"She paid ten thousand dollars for the baby," I said. "I was already pretty sure of that. She probably doesn't know the background. But I'd bet money her husband does."

"Now what?" Kathy asked when I made no move to start the car.

"Now we wait," I told her. "We see how long it takes for Nick to get here."

It didn't take long. We waited maybe twenty minutes that must have felt like hours to Jackie Patten, until a Ford pickup screeched to a halt in front of the house. Jackie raced outside, her face distorted with tears, and a moment later a determined and angry-looking man who had to be Nick Patten was headed for the car where Kathy and I sat.

"Who the hell are you?" he demanded as I got out of the car. "And what the hell are you doing upsetting my wife?"

I showed him my identification.

"You're not in Fort Worth, bitch," he said.

"You like mine better?" Kathy asked, shouldering her way between us. She was a good three or four inches taller than he was.

"All right," he said, "you're cops, now what the hell are you doing upsetting my wife, telling her you're going to take our baby—"

Kathy began to recite a Miranda warning, and he yelled, "Oh, shut up. What do you think you are, a television show?"

"You want to talk to us?" I asked.

"No, bitch, I want you to talk to me. Upsetting my wife— she's waited for that baby for so damn long—"

"Mr. Patten," I said softly, "I understand a wait like that. My children are adopted. And last night somebody tried to kill my son to stop me from going farther on this case. Not give him back to his original parents, Mr. Patten, kill him. With a shotgun."

"Oh, come off it," he tried to laugh. "Nobody's that dumb, and anyhow, what do you mean, *this case*? Jackie already told you the baby's ours, we've got a birth certificate—"

"I don't doubt that for a second," I said. "I've seen the information from the computer printout. I know exactly what the birth certificate says. You want to answer some questions for me?"

"I'll answer any question you want."

"Where was the baby born?"

"In Fort Worth."

"Where in Fort Worth?"

"We—um . . ." He paused. Jackie might have told him I'd already asked; he was deciding whether to stick to the same lie or try a new one; or else Jackie didn't tell him and he was wondering if I'd asked her and what she'd said. "LaQuinta," he finally said.

"Then how come the birth information says he was born in the unincorporated part of Tarrant County?"

"I guess the midwife screwed up. Why don't you ask her?"

"What's her name?"

"Strada. Rachel Strada."

"Is she black or white?"

"White. Actually I think she's sort of Mexican or something like that."

I wondered if he'd actually seen Rachel Strada. Clearly Jackie hadn't, but somebody had to hand over the baby to him.

"Where did you learn about Rachel Strada, to hire her?"

"From—from a guy. I don't remember his name; he was just talking about his wife had just had a baby and they'd had this midwife that was real good, and he gave me her phone number."

"Oh, this baby you'd been waiting for so long, after your wife had several miscarriages, was delivered by a midwife you heard about from a guy whose name you don't remember?"

"He said she was real good. Jackie had gotten scared of doctors."

"And he gave you her phone number."

"Yeah. I don't have anything to hide. Neither does Jackie. You just got her all upset."

"Then what's Rachel Strada's phone number, Mr. Patten?"

"I lost it."

"Oh you did."

"Yeah."

"Then where does she live?"

"I don't know. She drove to the motel."

"What does her car look like?"

"I don't know, she parked around the side." By now he had relaxed; his face had that smirk familiar to all cops, the look of the man who thinks he's getting away with something.

"When I find her—and I will find her, Mr. Patten—and when I explain to her just how big the case she's mixed up in is, and when she finds out the FBI is now in it too, and when she finds out she's broken a lot of federal laws and a lot of state laws, what do you think Rachel Strada is going to tell me then?"

"She's going to tell you she delivered my wife's baby," Nick Patten said, leaning on the side of the police car, grinning.

"No, I don't think that's what she's going to tell me, Mr. Patten," I said, "and I don't think you do either. So why don't you go in the house and talk with your wife about what to do next?"

What Nick Patten said was not polite, and it was a biological impossibility. Then he turned on his heel and stalked toward Jackie, who was waiting on the walk in front of the house. He put his arm around her shoulder and they went in the house together.

"I'm sorry for them," Kathy said.

"For her, anyway," I answered. "The problem is that probably half or three quarters of the time she'd be right. The black market baby *is* better off with parents who'd pay ten thousand dollars for it than with parents who'd sell it. But every now and then you get a situation like this. Or one where the buyers can't get a legal adoption because it's perfectly obvious they'd be crummy parents—or even, the buyer is some kind of pervert. Jackie *does* love that baby, and she'd be a terrific mother if she just weren't so damn scared. Nick . . ." I looked at the house again. "I'm not so sure about Nick."

"But they're both scared, Deb," Kathy said, "and I—don't think it's just of us."

"I don't either," I said. And thought of Hal.

□ 10 □

Of course I took some time to call the school again. Yes, Hal was there. Yes, they were sure; the principal had just had to confiscate his drinking straw, which he was using as a pea-shooter.

I went and had lunch with Kathy, just in time to keep my stomach from talking back to me again.

Returning to my office about one, I checked my phone messages and found Miss Jones from the Texas Department of Health hadn't called back. "Damn," I said; I needed badly to talk with her, to find out how to go about locating a specific midwife who wasn't in the phone book.

Damn the city's phone bill. I called Austin again. Miss Jones was out for lunch. Yes, she'd been given my message. Yes, they'd give it to her again. No, her secretary was still sick. No, there was no one else who could help me. They were sorry.

They weren't half as sorry as I was. Because I was 100 percent certain that Rachel Strada could lead me to whoever had dreamed up this whole scheme.

I wasn't paying any attention to what anyone else was doing, nor to the telephone, until someone shouted at me to grab it. Miss Jones, I thought eagerly, reaching for it.

"Stein, Arlington. I just got to thinking, Deb, you want us to put a tail on the Pattens in case they decide to make like bunnies?"

I hadn't thought of that. I didn't think they would run—I was pretty sure Nick Patten thought he'd snowed us—but I might be wrong. "Can you do it without them noticing?"

"Yeah, sure. There's a vacant house across the street we can get the key to. We'll put the tail on her, not him—from what we saw today, I'd say he won't go far without her."

That was probably true. And as distraught as Jackie Patten was, most likely we could tail her with a Mack truck and she wouldn't notice. "Yeah, Kathy, I'd sure appreciate it."

"I'll keep you posted if there's any action."

I thanked her and went and reported to Millner. "What are you doing about finding Strada?" he asked.

"I'm working on it, I'm working on it. How are our computer whiz kids doing?"

"They say they'll have it all entered by quitting time today."

"That's fast."

"Well, we did ask for people who could type."

Strada. Strada. No phone listed; I'd already checked that. Driver's license? Car registration? Tax rolls? Utilities? I called Dispatch and asked them to check the computers, and I asked the secretary to check with the utilities. A dispatcher called back ten minutes later—no vehicle registration, not on tax rolls, but she did, surprise, surprise, have a driver's license. It showed an address on Rosedale.

So of course I got my car keys and I got my walkie-talkie and I went out and got in the car to drive to the address on Rosedale. As I headed for the door, the secretary called, "Hey, Deb. That Rachel Strada hasn't got any utilities at all in her name. No gas, no electricity, no water, no phone, no nothing."

"Okay, thanks for checking," I said. The fact that she did have an address, but didn't have any utilities, could be interesting in a lopsided sort of way. Why *wouldn't* they be in her name? If it wasn't a utilities-paid place—and I didn't think it was going to be—maybe I'd better find out whose name they *were* in.

It was an old house, actually a garage apartment covered with gray asbestos siding. I went up the rickety outside staircase and knocked on the door. No answer. There was no sound of radio or TV; there were no lights on that I could see.

I headed back downstairs. A fat, shirtless Mexican sitting on a front porch across the alley holding a can of beer yelled, in unaccented English, "You lookin' for Rachel Strada?"

"Yeah, you know where she is?"

"Uh-uh, I ain't seen her in a coupla days. You don't look pregnant to me." The first hint of Spanish accent—the "don't" came out more like "don'."

"It's not for me," I temporized. "But I really do need to see her."

"Well, if it's, you know, like an emergency, Rosa Gonzales in the next block might can help you."

"I don't guess it's an emergency yet," I said lamely. "But I do wonder if Miz Strada is close by. Do you know if she left in a car or on foot?"

"I don' know how she left," he said. "She don' got no car. But somebody might could have come and got her. She jus' gone, far's I can see. Mus' be a tough one, she gone this long. Poor lady."

"Yeah, I guess it must," I agreed, gathering that the "poor lady" referred to the hypothetical patient.

"Me an' Lupe, we got thirteen," he said. "It's got where it don' take Lupe no time atall. Las' time Rachel din' get here even, an' her livin' nex' door. Firs' time it took all night. But two days—damn!" He shivered eloquently.

I decided I liked him even if he was fat and bare-chested and drinking beer at two-thirty in the afternoon. So I waved goodbye to him before I went and sat in the car, wondering what to do next.

I wasn't sure putting a stakeout on her house would be a very good idea. Anyway it would be conspicuous—in this neighborhood, I felt sure, everyone knew everyone. But I couldn't risk *not* putting a stakeout, because I needed to grab her as soon as she walked in the door, just in case she grew bunny feet. I was sure her employers were getting nervous—they'd made that plain enough.

For that matter, though, I had no way of being sure she hadn't already spooked and taken off, not unless I got a search warrant (for which I felt sure I could now demonstrate probable cause) and searched the apartment. But I didn't want to do that because if she hadn't run yet, that would spook her for sure.

I started to radio in, but then I decided I'd better not, just in case they were monitoring the police bands. By now I was sounding slightly paranoid even to myself, but there are enough Bearcat and other scanners around to outfit every criminal in town. I got back out of the car and returned to the fat, friendly beer drinker. This time I showed ID. His eyes widened. "Yeah?" he said eagerly. "You mean like on TV? *Cagney & Lacey?*"

"Sort of," I said. I'm not a television watcher and I'd never seen *Cagney & Lacey,* but I did have a vague idea it was about women detectives.

"You mean Rachel's done something?"

"Oh, no," I assured him. I really wasn't even sure I was lying; she could have been an unwilling, or even unwitting, tool. "No, I think something awful's happened to one of her patients, and we need her to help find out, but we can't seem to locate her. Part of the problem is that we've never seen her and don't know what she looks like. Could you give us some kind of a description?"

We'd gotten a general physical description from the driver's license bureau—we knew she was five feet tall (no weight figures, because weight is subject to change) and had brown eyes (no hair color, because hair is subject to change) and was thirty-seven years old. We needed something better than that.

"Oh, yeah, sure," he said. "You wan' my name? I'm Francisco Villas, they call me Pancho, get it, Pancho Villas? Like Pancho Villa?" I assured him I got it, and he said, "Well, now, Rachel.

Well, she's a short little thing, maybe two inches shorter than you?" I nodded; per Department of Public Safety records he was on the nose. "Thin, scrawny, you know, like a plucked chicken, nothing for a man to take to bed. Maybe that's why she don' got a man." He laughed uproariously at his own humor. "Lessee, black hair, she keeps it cut real short, brown eyes, clothes, well, she wears mos'ly dresses, no slacks, dark color dresses an' ol' lady shoes, you know what I mean." He shrugged. "Thass all, I don' know what else you want."

"I appreciate your help, Mr. Villas—"

"Pancho, Pancho!"

"Pancho then. Here's a card with my phone number on it. If you see her, here or anywhere, would you call my office? And don't tell her; I don't want her to get scared."

"Yeah, I gotcha." He took the card and put it in his pants pocket and looked at me shrewdly. I was very much afraid he understood more than I wanted him to. But I'd had to get a description somewhere, and although he didn't look like the most industrious human being in the universe, he did look reasonably honest.

I know. Famous last words. But you have to trust somebody, even in this crazy, screwed-up world.

I went to the closest 7-Eleven, bought a Coke and a package of potato chips and a box of antacids, and called in. Gary said he'd get me a stakeout. I said I'd meet him out there. I took the time then to call the school. Hal had left with Sammy Cohen. Yes, they were sure. They saw him get in the truck.

I went back and sat in front of the apartment, fretting about the time I was wasting and wishing I'd thought to ask Gary to have Ellen check to see whose name the utilities were in, and after about forty-five minutes a rattletrap blue Mercury I recognized as belonging to our intelligence unit wheezed up. It choked and died (aided, I was sure, by a switch on the dash) only seconds after pulling up behind me. Ernesto Rubacava got out, dressed like a Latin American pimp complete with patent leather shoes and too-wide pants with a crease you could shave with, and opened the hood. He looked under it disgustedly and then sauntered over to me, a brown Mexican cigarette drooping from one corner of his mouth. "Hey, lady, you got a wrench?" he asked loudly, and then muttered, "Which house?"

"The gray garage apartment." I made like I was looking in the glove box. "Ernie, you look like hell."

"So I'm supposed to. Hey, lady, most people keep wrenches in the trunk."

"You think I'd get out of my car for somebody who looks like you?" I muttered, and then swung the car door open.

With both of us leaning over the trunk, he asked, "Description?"

I gave it, fast, and he got a wrench out of the trunk. I followed him to the front of his car. "Ernie, grab anybody who tries to get into that apartment." I watched him industriously loosen and then tighten two or three nuts or valves or whatever they were—I have never claimed to be a mechanic—and then said, "Look, mister, I've got to go, so you've got to give my wrench back."

He stalked back to my trunk, pitched the wrench into it, slammed the trunk, glared at me, and headed disgustedly back to his engine, stopping on the way to kick a tire.

Out of the corner of my eye, as I started my car, I could see Pancho Villas sitting on his front porch laughing. If he was any sharper, he'd cut himself, I thought, and hoped he didn't know how to reach Rachel. But illogically, I felt if he knew he'd have told me.

In the office I found Miss Jones still hadn't called back. But the computer entries were completed, and one of the borrowed patrolmen had even walked over to the city hall to pick up the printouts of the sorted information.

I was ready to look at it and see what I could piece together, but it was four o'clock and Captain Millner was wandering from room to room saying, "Day watch, beat it, head for the barn!" I snatched up the stack of printouts and headed for the door.

"Where do you think you're going with those?" Captain Millner demanded.

"With what?" I asked blandly, staring at him wide-eyed—a technique which has served me in good stead in some places, but has totally failed to impress Captain Millner.

He looked at me for a moment and then shook his head. "I don't see a thing," he said. "Don't forget your walkie-talkie." He strode past me and out the door.

I went out to the farm and picked up Hal, who'd had an uneventful afternoon of riding on a borrowed horse and herding the milk cows up to the barn. The cows would have gone to the barn quite as well without his help, but that was beside the point; he was quite pleased with himself and chattered all the way home about the merits of buying a horse, and it was okay that we couldn't keep it in Summerfields because it could live at Sammy's house.

Summerfields, I should belatedly explain, is a suburb of Fort Worth *and* a suburb of Keller. That is, it is inside the city limits of Fort Worth, which subjects it to city taxes and city regulations (including no horses on a quarter-acre lot), but it is in the Keller Independent School District. Which may or may not be *better* than Fort Worth schools, but it's certainly *smaller*, and that for my money is an advantage.

After I got home last night, Harry went back out to the wrecking yard and retrieved the groceries, and they were now—all except the refrigerator and freezer stuff, which he had put away—still sitting on the kitchen table waiting for me. I hadn't even noticed them last night or I'd have put them away then; I was so frantic for something to do to work off my nervous energy that I even sorted out the linen closet, a task I perform only about once a year and only when it has become totally impossible to find a towel without knocking three sheets out onto the floor.

I put the groceries away. I started a salmon loaf for supper, got out some frozen green peas to serve with it, and started the water for rice. And heard Pat growling.

Pat does not normally growl except at the mailman, and the mailman does not come at five o'clock in the afternoon. I went to the door with my pistol in my hand.

The UPS man, standing on the other side of the fence staring at the gate with the large snarling dog just inside it, yelped and jumped back. When I hastily lowered the pistol, he grinned weakly and said, "Gee, lady, I know *dogs* don't like me, but—"

"I'm sorry, I thought it might be someone else," I said lamely. Setting the pistol on a bookcase by the front door, I walked out and corralled Pat, putting him on a running line before I went to the gate and signed for the package. I then unleashed Pat, retrieved my pistol, went in the house, and said, "Hal."

"Yes, ma'am?" That was a yes-ma'am tone of voice I had just used.

"Did you join a record club?"

"Well, I—"

"Did you join a record club?"

"I can pay for it!"

"How?"

"By mowing lawns," he protested, and I pointed out to him that it was nearly October and there is no lawn mowing to be done between October and March. Nor, in Fort Worth, is there any snow shoveling to fill in with.

"Well, if you'll pay for the records now, I'll pay you back when—"

"Hal," I said, "your father and I both distinctly told you not to join a record club."

"Aw, Mom!"

"Didn't we?"

"Yeah, but—"

"The records go back." I took them off to my bedroom, which is protected from marauding kids when I'm not home by a deadbolt on the inside door, and put the records on a closet shelf. Actually I had no intention whatever of returning them—Hal had a birthday in about two weeks, and at least this was something I was 100 percent sure he wanted. I'd just have to intercept the record brochures between now and next March, to see to it he didn't order something he had no way of paying for.

He went to his room, sulking, and then emerged ten minutes later to ask if he could go over to Andy's and watch television.

"We have a television," I said, "and Andy is perfectly welcome to come over here."

"Aw, Mom!" he protested. "Our TV hasn't . . ." He stopped, looking guilty.

"I know. Our television hasn't got MTV on it. Hal, come sit down." I perched on the arm of the couch, and he slouched over, looking offended, and sat down by the opposite arm, as far from me as he could get and still be on the couch. "Hal," I said, "I know things are going to be pretty boring for you for a while. But whoever shot at us last night is still wandering around somewhere, and he could try again. Hal, I've got to see to it you're protected and safe, even if you do get mad at me for it."

"Then will you at least get MTV back?"

"No, I won't, Hal. I've already told you the reason for that." Actually there was a way he could get MTV, but I wasn't about to tell him. The only way to lock MTV off is with a gadget on the cable box; it locks the sound off but not the picture, and most radios of the kinds kids like now—the so-called "ghetto blaster" variety of which Hal now had two—will pick up television sound. But the longer Hal didn't know that, the better satisfied I would be.

"Aw, Mom, there's nothing to *do* around here!"

"Books. Records. Tapes. Television. The VCR. Your weight-lifting stuff in the garage. Magazines. That guitar you were going to lie down on the floor and die if I didn't get you."

"It's at Andy's."

"What's it doing there?"

"I left it there. Can I go get it?"

"No, but you're welcome to invite Andy to come over here."

He sighed deeply and then brightened. "Can I invite Andy to spend the night?"

"Not tonight. It's a school night."

"Friday's not a school night!"

"This isn't Friday; it's Thursday."

"Mom, it's Friday!"

I picked up the newspaper and looked at the date. He was right. It was Friday. I knew I was tired, but I didn't know I was that tired. "Yeah, Andy can come over."

"Can I invite Sammy too?"

All right, I am a sucker. By the time I got through—or he got through—we were having Andy *and* Sammy *and* Steve *and* Robert *and* Ted to spend the night and I had been suckered into agreeing to pizza for the multitude as a midnight snack. Hal went off to his room whistling and I returned to the salmon loaf.

Hal said he didn't want any of it. He'd wait for the pizza. He slipped past me, not as invisible as he thought he was, with a bag of potato chips in his hand.

That was okay. There were two bags on my dresser. "Hal," I said.

"Yeah?"

"There are some Fritos too."

"Oh. Okay." He sauntered back to the pantry and got the Fritos.

It was just as well he didn't want any of the salmon loaf. I didn't have enough to feed six teenage boys.

By the time Harry and I finished supper—Becky, we gathered from a rather incoherent telephone call, was infesting Olead's kitchen—the rock music from the middle bedroom was much too loud for me to concentrate on printouts. In fact, I had begun to fear nobody was going to get any sleep tonight. But Harry said, "They can keep it on till midnight. After that it goes off."

In fact, I was asleep well before midnight. At nine-thirty Harry called Domino's to deliver the pizza instead of taking off in the truck to get it; maybe he was more nervous than I had realized. But with the assurance I wasn't going to be the only adult in the house, I went to sleep despite the racket.

I awoke sometime during the late night. I knew it was late because even the giggling from Hal's room had stopped; it might have been 3:30 or 4 A.M. And Pat was barking his head off.

Pat barks at people. He does not bark at the wind; he does not bark at other dogs unless they get in our yard; he does not bark at cats; and he does not bark at people he knows except the mail carrier. He barks at strangers. But if they're just passing by on the street, he barks only perfunctorily, to let them know he knows they're there. When he barks like he was barking now, he's barking at a stranger in the yard.

I turned the light on and reached for my pistol. "You can't go out like that," Harry protested, and I said, "Why not? I'm covered."

"Barely." He threw me a housecoat, and I clutched it around me with my left hand because my right hand was full of pistol and I didn't want to take the time to button.

But before I got out the bedroom door, the front porch light went on and boys poured out the front door, yelling, "A burglar! Hal's got a burglar!"

I heard a loudly profane voice in the front yard, and then a motorcycle started up. By the time I got out the door, he was gone. If the boys hadn't spooked him, I'd have had him. And of course they were all far too excited to have noticed what he looked like.

I went back to the bedroom and threw myself on the bed and burst into tears.

□ 11 □

I N RETROSPECT, it's really rather embarrassing. I couldn't seem to stop crying. Becky came in and tried to comfort me by offering me Kleenex and cuddling me. Hal, looking embarrassed as only a teenage boy can, said, "Mom, I'm sorry, I didn't know you didn't want us to go outside."

"I'm not mad," I choked, and grabbed for more Kleenex.

"Everybody out," Harry said from the bedroom door. "She's just tired." He came in and provided a shoulder. I don't remember when I stopped crying, but it was nearly noon before I woke up with my stomach doing its now-familiar tango. Cravenly I ate potato chips from a bag I had left beside the bed before I got up, and then went into the living room.

The extraneous teenagers had gone home. Becky at some time earlier in the morning had made muffins, and their crumby remnants were stuck to the muffin pans sitting on top of the stove; she was now perched on the couch watching cartoons with Jeffrey on her lap. Hal, for the moment scornful of such kid stuff, was playing chess with Olead. Harry, sitting at the ham radio, was listening to two men in Louisiana chaff each other about the relative lack of merit of each other's coon dogs.

Everybody looked at me, nervously.

"Good morning," I said.

"Good morning," Harry said.

Nobody said anything else. I suppose they were all waiting to see if I was going to start crying again. I felt ridiculous.

Trailing the remnants of my dignity, I went into the kitchen and managed to chisel three of the muffins out of the muffin pan and butter them—luckily the margarine had been left out of the refrigerator and was quite soft—and I got a glass of milk and went back to the living room, trying to avoid spilling crumbs on my printouts. That proved to be impossible if I was eating while I was reading the printouts, so I decided I had better take them in order. I put the printouts down, finished the muffins, and went and actually did the dishes. All of them. Without asking Harry or the kids to help me. I washed them and I dried them and I put them away and I put everything back where it belonged—that took a while—and I washed all the countertops and the tabletop and the top of the microwave and I put a roast in the Crockpot for dinner. I even remembered to put the potatoes and carrots in before the roast, which is the way you do it if you're cooking the roast in the Crockpot.

I wandered through the living room to find Harry staring at me in open amazement. He looked away quickly when he noticed I'd noticed.

I gathered up the dirty laundry and sorted it into three stacks—whites, light-colored, and dark-colored. Usually I stuff a single load of everything except Hal's jeans into the washer at the end of every day, but I hadn't been doing that this week and things had sort of gotten away from me. I put the first load into the washer and went and stripped the beds. All of them. Even Becky's.

"Deb, are you feeling okay?" Harry asked.

"Yeah, sure," I said absently, sticking several days' accumulation of newspapers into a black plastic trash bag.

Harry turned the radio off and stood up. "What are you doing?" I asked.

"Well, if you're that ambitious, I guess I better go mow the lawn," he said. "Anyhow if I get it now, I won't have to mow it again till spring. Hal, grab the Weed Whacker."

Hal glanced at me before he went out the door. But if he wasn't safe in the front yard with his father in broad daylight, he wouldn't be safe anywhere.

"Mom, can I help you?" Becky asked.

"No, thank you, I'm fine," I said absently.

"Then you can come help me," Olead said. "Seems to me *my* kitchen is a wreck and a disaster." He scooped up a giggling Jeffrey under his arm and headed for the front door; Becky grabbed her purse and followed him.

Well, I thought lugubriously two hours later, if one of us gets killed, at least we'll have a clean house for the funeral.

I couldn't imagine what had gotten into me. There is nobody in the world who detests housework quite as much as I do; I do it only because it has to get done and nobody else seems eager for the task; but for some inexplicable reason I had actually done tons and acres and bales of it with no coercion at all, in record time at that.

Finally, unable to think of anything else to do except wash the windows or shampoo the carpet—I wasn't that eager to do housework—or defrost the freezer, which is Harry's job because it is a chest freezer and with me the size I am it is totally impossible for me to scrub the freezer without getting inside it, which doesn't seem like a very good idea, I went back to my printouts.

Harry and Hal came in, dirty and sweaty and looking enormously pleased with themselves, and headed for both bathrooms, to engage in a shouted and acrimonious debate over the use of the water which ended when Harry yelled, "Hal, I said *turn it off* until I'm through."

I ignored them and read printouts.

I had asked to have the records sorted by the name of the person delivering the baby, and I was looking for Rachel Strada. Unfortunately, I had not asked to have the names of doctors and midwives sorted alphabetically. There are a lot of people who deliver babies in Tarrant County.

There it was, Rachel Strada. The Pattens, yes, I knew about them. Rachel Strada had also delivered the babies of Edward and Irene O'Neal, Dean and Catherine Norris, Gerald and Sarah Thompson, Richard and Connie Hughes, and Lyndon and Victoria Scott. All births had occurred during a span of time stretching from March to the first week of September, and they all had taken place in the unincorporated areas of Tarrant County.

The other thing I wanted to look for now was any family having registered two births in a period of less than nine months, but it belatedly occurred to me that in order to check on that I should have gotten records going back to January instead of only back until March. Somehow I didn't think I was going to be very popular Monday morning, that is unless I could manage to clear this up over the weekend.

Dirty Harry can clear up a case in two hours. But I'm not Dirty Harry, and I didn't expect Captain Millner would be very happy if I started trying to clear this case with a .44 Magnum. Or even with a .38 special.

I started taking notes. The O'Neal baby was a five-pound seven-ounce girl. The Norris baby was a seven-pound four-ounce boy. The Thompsons had a nine-pound fourteen-ounce —ouch, I thought—boy. The Hughes baby was an eight-pound two-ounce girl. And the Scotts had a six-pound ten-ounce boy.

Now if I could find them . . .

The telephone book gave me an Edward O'Neal on University Drive in Fort Worth, a Dean Norris on El Dorado in North Richland Hills, a Gerald Thompson on Timber Terrace in Arlington, a Richard Hughes on Regent Row in Benbrook, and a Lyndon Scott on River Oaks Boulevard in Fort Worth.

They might or might not be the ones I was looking for. Only time would tell that.

Okay, O'Neal and Scott were in my own jurisdiction; I could go after them by myself. Thompson was in Arlington; I could get Kathy on it. For Norris I'd have to get an assist from the North Richland Hills PD, and for Hughes I'd have to talk to the Benbrook department.

I wondered where that phrase "get an assist" came from. It sounded awful.

Saturday. I wasn't even supposed to be on duty.

Damn the Supreme Court anyway, I thought not for the first time. They thought they were helping us when they ruled that police had to be paid for every second of overtime from now on. And I guess in the long run they were. But the cities hadn't budgeted for that kind of load, and the result was that people were getting called not only off of routine traffic details but also off of homicides, nationwide. And police officers like me sometimes wound up clandestinely trying to work from home and hoping they wouldn't get caught at it.

Okay, so what could I do that was simple and fast?

A long time ago, when I was very young and not married yet, I sold magazine subscriptions over the telephone for a while. I hadn't forgotten how. I grabbed the most recent Publisher's Clearing House You May Have Already Won to get an idea of current prices—I'd be selling *Parents* magazine, I decided. That would give me a reasonable pretext for asking if there was a baby in the house. I didn't wonder what I'd do if any of them decided to buy the magazine—people don't usually. It's really a tough way to make a living.

The Edward O'Neals did not want to buy a magazine. I was wrathfully informed that anybody who would call during a baby's naptime was a jerk anyway.

There was no answer at the Norris household.

When I dialed the Thompsons' number, I got a recording referring me to a telephone number in the 213 area code. That's interesting, I thought—213 is Los Angeles.

Mrs. Hughes told me yes, she had a baby, yes, she had all the magazines she wanted, please leave her alone.

When I dialed the Scotts' number, I got a recording that said, "We are sorry, you have reached a number that is no longer in service."

"Deb," Harry asked, "what do you think you're doing?"

"Trying to find something out," I said. "If I go somewhere, will you keep an eye on Hal?"

"Aw, Mom!" Hal protested.

"I will be very happy to keep an eye on Hal," Harry said pleasantly. "I also will be very happy to keep an eye on the front yard and the backyard. I should have done this a couple of days ago." He took his shotgun off the gun rack, loaded three shells into it, and added, "Hal, if you touch this, I promise to flay you."

"What does 'flay' mean?"

"Look it up in the dictionary. Are you supposed to be doing that?" he added to me.

"No," I said.

"I just wanted to know."

"Now you know."

I went out the door and stopped short. Parked half a block from my house, on the edge of the vacant field where the fire department sometimes likes to come and hold maneuvers, was an unmarked car. But it was a perfectly recognizable unmarked car, to me and probably to anybody who shouldn't be recognizing it, because the two whip antennas were a little conspicuous and so was the high-priced, high-powered car without a scrap of trim. I walked over to it.

"Hi," Bill Livingston said.

"What are you doing here?"

"After your little contretemps last night, Millner thought you might better have a little protection."

"I can look after myself, thanks."

"So where are you going?"

"Out. Does it matter?"

"Not especially. My orders are to look after the house and whoever's in it."

"Look, this is absurd."

"Don't blame me," Bill said, "blame Millner. Look, Deb, from what I've heard, it sounds to me like you might be playing in the big leagues now."

"That is a distinct possibility."

"So who's still in the house? It would help to know."

"My husband. My son. The cars that belong here, besides my car and Harry's truck, are Becky's Toyota, my son-in-law's Escort—it's red—and Olead Baker's Ford van. Anything else you might want to check on. There are always teenagers in and out, but any adults you don't know who don't fit those cars you might check on."

"Will do. Does the dog bite?"

"Not unless you're in uniform. Actually he never has bitten that I know of, but he barks at people in uniform. He thinks they're all the mail carrier and he hates the mail carrier."

"Yeah?" Bill drawled, looking puzzled.

I didn't ask why he looked so puzzled.

That was a mistake.

Irene O'Neal was home alone; her husband was at work. "He works most of the time," she said wistfully. "He's hardly ever home. He's a lot older than me, you know. He's fifty-seven."

Irene was not more than about twenty-two. She was a sweet-faced girl, poorly educated and, I suspected, not overly intelligent. I had introduced myself, but I wasn't sure she'd understood. "Mrs. O'Neal," I began, and recited a Miranda warning.

"I don't know what all that means," she said vaguely. I started to explain, but she said, "Oh, no, don't bother, I don't mind talking with you. You wanted to ask questions about Junie, didn't you? We call her Junie because she was born in June, isn't that cute? Thing is, I didn't have anything to do with it. I can't have babies." There was desolation in her voice. "My mother took some kind of medicine before I was born and it made me have a lot of trouble and the doctor said I had to have a hysterectomy so I wouldn't get sicker. So I can't have babies. And I felt real bad about it. So Eddie told me to quit whining, he'd get me one. And he said he'd take care of all the details and everything. He said all I'd have to do was get things ready, and he asked me if I'd rather have a boy or a girl and I thought maybe he'd rather have a boy but he said no, whatever I wanted, and so I said I'd like a girl because they're so much fun to dress, and so he said then get ready because the first girl that's available we'd get, and I got the baby's room all ready and sure enough along came Junie. Isn't she cute?"

She was a doll. She had a rosebud mouth, reddish brown curls, blue eyes, pink cheeks. At three months she was definitely taking an interest in her surroundings, and Irene hugged her happily.

"I'm the oldest of nine," she added, "and everybody thought I never would want any kids of my own because I've had to look after so many, but I just can't imagine not having a baby around to cuddle."

Somebody else was going to have to tell Irene Junie wasn't hers. I had just decided I wasn't going to be the one to do it.

"You say Eddie took care of all the arrangements?"

"Oh, yeah, I didn't even have to fill out any papers or anything. He even got them to fix it so the birth certificate says I had her, so she never will even find out she's adopted. Except I think I ought to tell her anyway, don't you? I mean, she ought to know she had a mom before me. That must take a lot of courage, giving a baby away because you know you can't take care of it right. I'm not sure I could. I'm afraid I'd keep it and just try to do my best, but that might be pretty rotten for the baby, if the situation was, you know, wrong, kind of. I'd like to meet her birth mother sometime, just to thank her, you know."

"Where does Eddie work?" I asked.

She looked puzzled suddenly, and worried. "You know, I don't know? He told me this place he said he was working, and he told me never to call him at work because he was real busy, but I called there anyway this morning because he got a phone call at home that they said was real urgent, and that place where he said he worked, they told me they'd never heard of him. You'd think I'd know anyway, but he and I met in a club, you know, where I was working, and he said I was a pretty little doll he'd like to take home in his pocket, and I said was his pocket big enough, and he said, baby, I'll make it big enough. You'd think he would tell me where he works, wouldn't you, in case I needed to get in touch with him in case of an emergency or something. I wonder why he lied about it?"

"Where'd he tell you he worked?" I asked. That might at least give me a clue as to how his mind worked.

"A restaurant. In Tandy Center. He told me he runs it. But he doesn't." She told me the name of the restaurant. I knew it well—more bar than restaurant actually, but a pleasant place that serves a spinach salad I particularly like. I know the manager. His name is not Eddie O'Neal.

Irene, I thought, you're a nice girl, but you're not right bright. I stood up. "Thank you," I said, "you've been a lot of help."

"Was that all you wanted to know?"

"I might need to get back with you later," I evaded.

"That's okay, I'll be right here. Me and Junie, we just don't go places."

Not quite sure why I was doing it, I gave her my telephone number.

At the first pay phone I called Intelligence, intending to ask what they knew about Eddie O'Neal. But there was no answer at their phone.

Of course, I thought, they too have the order not to work overtime.

I called home. Harry said everything was okay and asked if I knew we were now the subject of a stakeout. I told him I knew it.

Which reminded me of the stakeout I'd set up. I drove over on Rosedale. Carlos Amado—the name means Charles Lover, which has gotten him a lot of kidding from his colleagues—was now sitting in front of Rachel Strada's apartment. He told me there had been no activity there. My friend Pancho, no more and no less drunk than yesterday, waved his can of Carta Blanca at me and shouted, "Hola!"

I waved and drove off, stopping at a 7-Eleven to get a can of Sprite. I was unaccountably thirsty.

We had, of course, placed a lookout statewide for Rachel Strada, but we didn't expect the lookout to accomplish anything. I was beginning to doubt that the stakeout was going to accomplish anything either. If she wasn't home by Monday, I'd get a search warrant and go on in—I'd do it Sunday if it weren't for that idiotic no-overtime rule.

The Norrises were in North Richland Hills and the Hugheses were in Benbrook. It would not be politic to go asking for aid from neighboring departments, not when I was officially off duty. The Thompsons seemed to have moved to Los Angeles; well, at least I could go by the office in a few minutes and have a Teletype sent to Los Angeles. Even with the no-overtime rule (which might not have hit them; Los Angeles is a rather wealthy town) they were bound to have people on duty all the time.

The Scotts lived on River Oaks if they were still there—the phone call wasn't conclusive. I headed that way.

They had, I discovered, changed their telephone number because phone calls kept waking the baby, to Mrs. Scott's great annoyance.

I couldn't imagine a greater contrast than that between Irene O'Neal, who deserved better than she was going to get, and Victoria Scott, who in my possibly biased opinion deserved worse.

The house was big, old, beautifully furnished, and dark. The baby—a six-pound ten-ounce boy, as I recalled—howled steadily at the back of the house, while Victoria Scott sat stiffly in the living room. "I feed him on a schedule," she told me. "It wouldn't do for him to get spoiled. No, that wouldn't do at all. He must grow up properly equipped to take his place in society."

"It's not spoiling babies to cuddle them a little," I said, and she sniffed disapprovingly.

"Just why are you here, Miss . . . What did you say your name was?"

"Detective Ralston," I said, "and I'm here to talk with you about a suspected violation of the law." I recited her a Miranda warning. She sniffed again. "Are you willing to talk with me?"

"I most certainly am *not*," she replied. "The very idea, suspecting people of our stature in society of some petty little crime! I shall contact my attorney at once and notify him of this outrage."

"I'm sure you will, Mrs. Scott," I said. "I'm sure you will. While you're at it, you might ask him to explain to you the meaning of the term 'party to a crime.'"

"And just what do you mean by that?"

"That if, as I suspect, a woman was murdered so that her baby could be sold to you, you just might be considered an accessory to murder."

"*Really!*" she snorted. "I'll have you know I'm a good Christian woman and I have never heard such an outrageous thing in my life. I suggest you leave my house at once before I summon the police."

"You don't seem to understand, Mrs. Scott," I said as I stood up. "I *am* the police. Or at least one of them."

She saw me to the door, her expression eloquent of utter contempt, and I sat in my car for a minute, choking with rage. Then, belatedly, I realized what I should have realized in the house. Nobody acts the way Victoria Scott was acting, no matter how wealthy or nouveau riche she is, unless she's putting on a show. Unlike Irene O'Neal, possibly unlike Jackie Patten, Victoria Hughes knew exactly what she'd done. She was terrified— and she was prepared to fight me with everything she had.

In her case, "everything" included all the clout a lot of money and a lot of family connections could bring to bear. The exaggerated pompousness, as if she'd been reading lines in a bad play, had been no more than the first warning rattle.

I knew I wasn't on duty. But it wouldn't hurt just to go by the office and check the top of my desk.

Dutch Van Flagg was frowning over a stack of paper on which he was industriously drawing diagrams, apparently trying to work out who was where at any given time. "Hi, Dutch," I said, "I didn't know you were working today."

"I'm not. I'm tilting at windmills. How'd you get approved to work?"

"I didn't." I burped loudly and grabbed a package of potato chips out of my desk drawer to go with the Coke I'd bought downstairs.

Dutch stared at me. "If I didn't know better, I'd swear you was pregnant," he told me.

"Ha-ha," I retorted. "It's another ulcer." I started sorting papers. On top of my desk was a Teletype from the chief of detectives in Lawton, Oklahoma. He'd heard I was working a case involving kidnapped pregnant women. He wanted me to know he had two: Dana Carlisle, gone since September 9, who had a baby due October 2, and Petra Kent, missing since August 23, whose baby was due the end of September.

I hadn't even thought of checking out of state. Now I called Dispatch and asked for more Teletypes—Oklahoma, Arkansas, Louisiana. I thought about it a moment and called back and told him to add Kansas. It's not really all that far to Kansas.

"How about if I make it nationwide?"

I guessed that was okay, although I didn't think our apparently localized gang had been kidnapping anybody from Oregon or Vermont.

That done, I called Lawton. Of course they're afflicted by the same Supreme Court decision we are, and there was only one person on duty in their detective office at the moment. He told me his name was Ted Two Tails and he could do without any jokes, thank you. He had a little more information than the Teletype gave me; what it boiled down to was that Dana and Petra were both respectable married women. Dana was expecting her first baby, Petra her third. They'd both been taken from the parking lot of the same grocery story about nine-thirty at night, apparently at random. Both cars had been left there and both purses were in the car.

Prompted a little more, he added that they were both Caucasian and yeah, judging from their pictures, you could call them pretty.

That fit. All the women had been pretty. The gang wanted pretty babies; they must have figured you get them from pretty mothers.

Lawton, Ted added, was pretty hysterical. That sort of thing didn't happen there. When the first one broke, they thought maybe some Army guy from Fort Sill had gone berserk; the second had brought dark murmurs from the Anglo lunatic fringe about secret Indian blood rituals. He hoped we could help.

That sort of thing, I told him, shouldn't happen anywhere, and I hoped he could help me. I asked for photocopies of everything they had. He said he'd send them, but there just wasn't much.

It wasn't until after I'd hung up that it hit me—this makes it interstate for sure. It's a federal case now.

I called the FBI—they liked to work a five-day week even before the Supreme Court started playing games with police schedules, but there's usually somebody on duty.

The somebody—a sweet young thing who set my teeth on edge with her condescension to a mere local cop—told me she'd get in touch with Agent Arnold and have him call me.

While I was waiting, I set about drawing a chart of my own. Maybe I was prompted by watching Dutch, but it seemed a new idea was trying to coalesce in my mind and I was trying to think of a way to get at it. I'd made a lot of charts earlier in the week, trying to work out any possible resemblance these women might have to one another, but this one got into an area I hadn't really thought about too carefully.

When I got through, I knew that pending any more reports from other towns I had one woman kidnapped in March, one in

June, four in July, five in August, and two in September. That meant that either they were beginning to gear down—which I didn't expect for a minute—or the murder of Grace Hammond had shaken them—which was another thing I didn't believe for a moment—or I could expect to hear from a few more towns.

And I knew that as far as I could tell now, there was one baby due in April, one in July, four in August, five in September (not counting Grace) and one in October.

Rachel Strada had delivered six babies. We had to have at least one more midwife involved.

Dana Carlisle almost certainly hadn't had her baby yet. Petra Kent and Katherine Irving, both due in very late September, might not have had theirs yet.

Somewhere, within walking distance of my house, there were some unmarked graves. I was already sure of that. But more important, there was at least one terrified woman, and quite possibly three or more, waiting, crying, praying for help.

For my help?

The phone rang. Quite automatically I answered it. "Deb," Captain Millner said, "go home."

"But—"

"Deb. Go home. Now. I didn't make the rule and I think it's a crappy rule, but it's still a rule. Go home. Who else is up there?"

I pointed at Dutch and he picked up the phone. I put mine down. In a minute I heard Dutch saying, disgustedly, "Yes, sir."

He started gathering his papers together.

I was way ahead of him. My printouts were already at home. And anyway it was right at four o'clock.

Only the telephone rang.

□ 12 □

DUTCH AND I both grabbed the phone at the same time. "We're not on duty," Dutch said.

"Sure you are," the dispatcher chirped. "You got a murder, you lucky, lucky people."

"We aren't Homicide," I said.

"No, but you're *there*."

"Where's the corpse?" Dutch asked resignedly.

"And *who's* the corpse?" I added.

The dispatcher gave an address. "It's some doctor," he said. Speaking away from the phone, he added, *"Yeah, I've got Ralston and Van Flagg. Okay, I'll tell them."* Back with us, he said, "Your captain says you're on duty. The victim's name is Frank Kirk. His wife just came home and found him laying in the middle of the floor. ME and EMS are en route."

It wasn't the kind of house you'd expect a doctor to have. It had three bedrooms, but they were small bedrooms, and the added-on den looked like a do-it-yourself project. It had brick walls inside and out, but the mortar hadn't been put in quite straight or else the ground had settled, and now big cracks were radiating from both upper corners of the fireplace.

The den was where Kirk was lying, in khaki pants and a Marine Corps green T-shirt. He was on his back sprawled out with his head pointing into the room, slightly toward the kitchen, which meant that, standing, he'd apparently have been facing the sliding glass door that opened into the fenced backyard. A paper plate of potato chips and a plastic glass of milk had spilled all over the floor, so he'd been getting a snack, and a *TV Guide* was open on top of the TV. A perfectly ordinary man, on his way into the den to watch a ball game on TV.

He'd been shot once with a shotgun, and the shotgun hadn't been close to him.

The farther away a shotgun is, the more the pattern spreads.

Kirk was recognizable, but barely.

Mrs. Kirk was sobbing behind me, and I turned and led her back through the kitchen, into the formal living room, as the lab people crowded down the hall toward the den, leaving Dutch talking with an investigator from the medical examiner's office. This was another new one; I didn't know him and figured I'd meet him later. Right now I'd talk to—or rather, listen to—Mrs. Kirk.

"There was just no *reason*," she told me. "He didn't have any enemies." There's never any reason—that the wife knows, I thought as she paused to reach for Kleenex. "He was—he'd been—a Navy doctor, attached to the Marines the last few years he was in the service, and he retired and came to Fort Worth, and—and he said we'd live okay on his retirement pay, we didn't need a whole lot with the girls married and gone, and so he was working in an emergency room for a while and then one day he came home blazing mad about something and he wouldn't tell me what, and then he went and set up that clinic; he told me he'd try to help people who wouldn't get help any-where else, and—and—and— There was just no reason!"

From what he had told me, I was wondering whether I knew the reason. "Had he brought any paperwork home, any medical records, letters from patients, that kind of thing?"

She shook her head. "He always said—he said he didn't be-lieve in bringing your work home. He said that was the way to get ulcers." Well, that's the truth, I thought ruefully. "At home he liked to do carpentry work. And he read and took care of the yard and watched TV, just like anybody else."

"Did he ever mention a Grace Hammond?"

"Was that one of his patients?"

"Yes."

"Uh-uh. No, he never talked about his patients."

"Mrs. Kirk, can you think of—"

"All this happening so close together, it just doesn't make sense. Like—like somebody's got a *vendetta* against us or something!" She hadn't heard me at all. "People breaking in, and then that fire at the clinic, and now—"

"Breaking in?"

"Oh, yes, it was—"

"Breaking in here, or at the clinic?"

"Both! You mean you didn't know? But police came out here and took pictures and everything!"

"Well, burglary's worked by a different office," I explained. "I'll look up the report, of course, because there certainly could be a connection, but if you could just tell me a little about it now—"

"They had all the drawers open, I mean every drawer in the whole *house,* you just wouldn't believe what the place looked like, and—"

"That was here at the house?"

"Uh-huh."

"What did they get?" I asked. She'd stopped crying, at least temporarily.

"*Nothing!* That was the funny part—they made all that big mess, but they didn't take anything at all. At least if they did, it was nothing we missed."

"And the clinic? Someone broke in there too?"

"Oh, they didn't get in there."

"But you said—"

"They tried. But Frank had dead bolts and burglar bars, and they couldn't get in. I just—don't—know what they wanted. It doesn't make sense. It just doesn't make any sense at all."

Murder rarely does. But this was making a certain frail, tenuous amount of sense to me. If Grace had told her kidnappers somebody knew where she was, of course they'd go after the person she would have told. If you're running a murder mill, you can't afford to have anybody alive who knows where it is— at least not anybody you can't blackmail into silence.

She was crying again. I made conventional noises and got her a glass of water and an aspirin, which I guess was pretty stupid; would I want a glass of water and an aspirin if somebody had shotgunned Harry?

Or Hal?

But she took the aspirin and drank the water and said she guessed she'd go call her sister now. So I went back to the den. The ME's investigator had already left, and the lab people were wandering around in the backyard. There hadn't been much for them to do in the den—photographs, that was all, because about the best ballistics could do with a shotgun was try to figure out the distance from which it had been fired, and even that would be chancy unless they had the weapon.

There was no use dusting for fingerprints because all indications were that the killer had never entered the house.

Both Ident people and Dutch Van Flagg were clustered around something in a far corner of the backyard. I went to join them.

There was good grass all over the yard, but there'd been rain off and on during the week, and here was a hollow that apparently held a little water. Somebody had slid very heavily in the resultant black muck; I could make out enough to say it was a tennis shoe, but nobody'd ever be able to match it.

So goody goody gumdrop, now we probably knew where the perpetrator had come over the fence—the rough, zinc-coated hurricane fence that would never in a million years hold prints.

The fence backed up to an alley. Kirk had a corner lot. Across the cross street was the back parking lot and large Dempsty-Dumpster of a 7-Eleven. On the other side of Kirk's house the yard was waist-high in unmowed summer weeds and I'd seen the FOR SALE sign as we drove up.

The house back-to-back with Kirk's house had a two-car

garage on the back of its lot, and on both sides of the garage there was fencing overgrown with kudzu.

Theoretically Dutch and I should go and knock on doors and ask everybody if they'd seen a stranger in the neighborhood wandering around carrying a shotgun. A smoking shotgun, maybe.

I looked at Dutch. Dutch looked at me. We went and told the transport team they could have the body, and we got in Dutch's car and went back downtown. On the way I told Dutch what Kirk had told me, and what Mrs. Kirk had told me.

I didn't, of course, have to tell him someone also had come after *me* with a shotgun. That he knew full well.

He drove in silence. Then he said, "How did they know what Grace told the doctor?"

I was glad to see his mind was on the same track mine was. "My guess is, when she found out she was more likely to get six feet of dirt than five thousand or so dollars, she tried the old somebody-knows-where-I-went game. I— Oh, no, Dutch, stop at a pay phone!"

"Pay phone why?" he asked, turning into the parking lot of a 7-Eleven.

I didn't answer. I just ran for the telephone to gabble my telephone credit card number to the operator and put in a call to Sherman.

I was, of course, too late. Chief Ellis told me the old lady, Clara Hammond, had been found dead at ten-thirty that morning by the mailman. The official supposition was that she had surprised a burglar. He kind of doubted this himself, Ellis told me; burglars don't usually carry shotguns. At least not around Sherman.

He'd appreciate it if I'd keep him posted as the investigation progressed.

I was crying when I got back into the car to tell Dutch as much as I knew, as much as I had pieced together. And finally he said, "It's no wonder the Pattens are running scared then."

"What?" I said.

"The Pattens. From what you're saying, Jackie's got to be the one who told Grace who to contact."

Of course I'd figured that out a long time ago, but I'd let myself forget it. Yes, Nick knew what was going on, probably from the start, and Jackie most likely knew it too by now, but Jackie hadn't known to start with. It had to have been in complete innocence that Jackie told her friend where to reach somebody who might be willing to buy her baby for enough money to give her and Tim a fresh start.

Which said one or two halfway nice things about Jackie, maybe.

And then I said, "Dutch, there's one more person Grace might have told, one more person who might know—"

"So where do we send the meat wagon to now?"

"It might," I said, "be a little difficult to smuggle a shotgun into Huntsville State Prison."

I called Harry. Dutch called his wife, Alicia. I called Captain Millner. Dutch called Huntsville State Prison to let them know we were coming. And we took off in the detective car assigned to Dutch Van Flagg, heading over to Dallas to catch I-45 and drive to Huntsville.

At nine-thirty that night Dutch and I were sitting in a horseshoe-shaped reception area in the Huntsville Unit of the Huntsville State Prison, looking through a glass and mesh barricade at Tim Richards, convicted burglar and presumed father of the baby Grace didn't live to have.

He'd been crying, I could tell that from looking at him—he was blond, blue-eyed, fair-skinned, the kind of person crying really shows on. So he'd seen Grace as more than just a convenient female body, he'd cared about Grace, and that of course immediately made me a lot more disposed to care about Tim Richards.

Dutch told him what we wanted. His gaze shifted toward me. "Who're you?" he asked.

We'd told him once. I told him again, who I was and what I was.

"Okay," he said, not telling me I didn't look like a cop. "I don't see why you wanted to know what Grace was going to do that she didn't do. Grace is dead. What difference does it make now that she was going to let some rich dude adopt the baby? Look at me—do I look like supporting a baby? Do I want my kid to go on welfare? It would have been better for the kid, you ought to know that. But what difference does any of it make now? Grace is dead and the kid is dead and I wish to God I was dead too."

"Tim," I began, "Grace didn't know it, but the people she was going to—to let the baby go to—were killers. We think they killed her because she got away from them. And they killed a doctor she might have talked to, and they killed her aunt, and—"

"Miz *Hammond*? Some son of a bitch killed Miz *Hammond*?"

"Yeah," Dutch said, "and tried to kill this lady right here beside me, her and her son both."

"For what?" Tim demanded incredulously.

"Because once a habit of murder gets established, it gets easier and easier," I said. "Tim, we've got to know everything she told you about what she might do about the baby. Who she talked to, who she went to. Will you help us?"

"Yeah, but I just don't remember so much," Tim said. "Okay, first she was going to go to some doctor in Fort Worth and have him, you know, take the baby, and I told her she better not do any dumb thing like that or I'd kick her bottom so hard she never would sit down on it no more. And she told me she didn't really want to but she just didn't want to have no baby grow up like we growed up. Grace and me, neither one of us ever did have two cents to rub together, and it's no damn way to live."

He wiped his eyes with his right forefinger and thumb and went on. "Then later she called me and said this friend of hers and her husband had just adopted a baby and they'd paid this dude ten thousand dollars to arrange it, and the dude had told them five thousand of it went to the girl that'd had the baby and the rest of it was to pay doctors and lawyers and all. And Grace said if we had five thousand dollars, well, we'd have a *start*." That, of course, was exactly what I had surmised. "She said we could, when I got out of here, we could buy a car and get a place in Dallas where I could find a decent job, and the baby— the baby'd be okay, it'd have parents that really wanted it, and we'd have another baby later when we could take care of it, and—well, it made sense to me, you know?"

"Sure it did," I agreed. "So did she tell you where she was going?"

He shook his head. "Uh-uh," he said. "A place in Fort Worth, that's all she said. But why would she tell me more? I ain't never been to Fort Worth; if she'd give me an address, it wouldn't have meant nothing. But—there was one thing."

"Yeah?" Dutch said.

"I told her she better tell somebody where she was, in case she got in trouble. So she said that doctor she was going to go to, she said she already wrote him a letter about it, so he could tell the other girls if they wanted to go there."

"And he didn't tell you about the letter?" Dutch asked.

"He specifically said he never got one. She may have misaddressed it, or forgotten to mail it, or maybe she never even wrote it."

"Tim didn't say she was going to write it, though. He says she said she wrote it."

"So it got lost in the mail? I wonder where mail addressed to the clinic is going now? He must have filed a change of address with the post office."

It was certainly too late at night to call Mrs. Kirk and ask her. I didn't even go into the police station; Dutch dropped me by my car and I went straight home, to find Harry, at one-thirty in the morning, engaged in a rather innocuous conversation with a man in Russia.

"Undoubtedly KGB," Harry said happily as he turned off the radio. "I mean, who else in Russia would have a good ham radio?"

"A rich bureaucrat," I said, and yawned.

"How's your stomach?"

"Fine. I fed it antacids and milk and it was happy."

"Good. Let's put it to bed."

□ 13 □

I WENT TO CHURCH.

It wasn't especially that I wanted to, but Hal did, and it didn't seem to make much sense to drive half an hour each way to take him and then to retrieve him. It made a lot more sense just to stay there with him. Besides, I was kind of beginning to get used to the place.

That was why I didn't see the newspaper until nearly one o'clock.

I don't know how they found out. But there it was, outranking PROMINENT DOCTOR SHOT, a screamer headline visible on the paper thrown on the coffee table as soon as I walked in the door:

FORT WORTH BASE FOR MURDER FOR PROFIT
WOMEN MURDERED, BABIES SOLD? POLICE REFUSE COMMENT.

"Oh, shit," I said.

"Church does such wonders for your vocabulary," Harry said. "You should go every day."

"I can think of things a lot worse to say. Harry, *where* did they get that?"

"Danged if I know. Millner called here for you; I told him I'd have you call as soon as you got home."

"Is he at home or at the office?"

"He didn't say."

I tried the office first, on the theory that rules might not apply to captains. At least in this case I was right. Basically he wanted to ask me what I had just asked Harry—where did the press get the story? He didn't ask if our trip did any good; he'd already gotten that from Dutch.

I told him I didn't know, and he sighed. "Well, be thinking, because you've got an appointment with the reporters at three o'clock this afternoon."

His heart was not softened by my protest that I wanted to make fried chicken for supper; he told me I could stop by Colonel Sanders on the way home. So I'm allowed overtime to talk to reporters but not to work on the case, I thought but did not say. Instead I slammed into the kitchen, rattling pans unnecessarily loudly, until something caught my mind. "Harry," I asked, "do you know a magazine called *Mercenary Endeavor?*"

"Yeah, it's sort of an imitation *Soldier of Fortune*. I buy it because it has some pretty good articles about foreign military aircraft. Why?"

"Oh, because yesterday when Dutch was gathering all his stuff together, I noticed he had three copies of it tangled in with his printouts and notes."

"You sure he wasn't reading on his off time?"

"At the office on Saturday afternoon? Besides that, he was making a lot of notes—when I saw it first, I didn't know what it was because he had it opened to the classifieds."

"You want to look at the classifieds? I've got a couple of copies of it right here."

"Yeah." I came out of the kitchen, and Harry dug the magazines out of the pile of papers under his radio table. There were ads for T-shirts and caps. There were ads for books about knife fighting and survival after nuclear war and living off the land. (After a nuclear war? That sounded rather unlikely to me.) There were ads for free instructions for gun silencers, include $4.95 for postage and handling. There were ads for instructions on how to convert semiautomatic weapons into automatic weapons.

And then there were the personals.

Mercenary for hire, will go anywhere, do anything, for the right price.
Let a returned mercenary plan your company's international antiterrorist strategy. Expert in all phases of terrorism.
Explosives expert for hire at the right price.
Reply to Box 441, Mercenary Endeavor.

"Oh," I said. I should have guessed—Dutch was figuring if you didn't know anything about explosives and wanted a bomb made, this kind of magazine would be a good starting place.

"You found something?"

"I think I found out what Dutch was looking at." I handed Harry the magazine and pointed to the ad.

"Oh," Harry said, "well, yeah, you can find ads like that in *SOF* too."

"It ought not to be legal."

"That old Bill of Rights, Deb. Besides, he might be advertising to dynamite tree stumps in the north forty."

"Yeah, sure."

"What are you going to tell the reporters?" he asked.

"I don't know. Maybe I'll ask them to help find Rachel Strada. I don't know, Harry."

Becky was over at Olead's house again; I wish to goodness she'd just marry the boy and move on over, because this is getting ridiculous. Hal wandered through the house eating a peanut butter sandwich, and I could see the remnants of a ham sandwich and a glass of milk on the radio table. So the family could wait until I either went by Colonel Sanders or got home from the news conference and cooked supper. I went and got a ham sandwich for myself, and sat down with my printouts, looking at births recorded in the unincorporated area of Tarrant County by midwives.

Again there were more than I had expected. And I had

no probable cause, even in my own mind, to go and lean on all of these people even in the most tactful of ways, because almost all of them were exactly what they said they were, perfectly legitimate midwives and women who had very good reasons of their own for having their babies out of hospitals.

All the same, I was going to have to give careful instructions to my so-called task force, the members of which I had hardly even met yet, and Monday we were going to have to locate and talk with all of them we could.

And those we couldn't locate we'd need to look at even harder, to find out why they didn't want us to find them. With, probably, the help of the FBI.

And I still hadn't talked to Dub Arnold. If he'd returned my call yesterday—which he probably had; FBI agents are conscientious about such things—I wasn't in the office to get the call.

Well, I'd talk to him Monday.

I finished the ham sandwich, tried to keep my ears shut to the rock music from Hal's room, glanced at Harry, who was flipping through *TV Guide* trying to find out what channel had the best football game, and thought briefly about lying down on the couch and taking a nap.

Or maybe about getting out some yarn and crocheting. I didn't want to turn into a workaholic, and no matter how critical the situation was, I wasn't going to make it any better by making myself too tired to function.

I got as far as getting out the plastic file box I keep my yarn and crochet hooks in and wondering what I could do with leftover scraps of orange, green, maroon, and violet yarn, when the telephone rang.

Just as well. I couldn't really think of anything to do with them except give them to any convenient kid to use to make *ojos de Dios*, that interesting Mexican Christmas ornament made with yarn and small sticks.

"It's for you," Harry said.

Somehow I wasn't at all surprised.

Captain Millner said, "We've found Rachel Strada."

His tone implied quite a lot more than he said, and I replied, "Oh, shit. How?"

"Hit-and-run, in front of the Greyhound station last night. She didn't have any purse and she wasn't identified right away, but this morning somebody looking a little more carefully through her clothes found her driver's license in a pocket of her dress. Word just now got to me."

Nobody saw the car.

The wheel marks had been left by radial tires, big ones, the kind that might be on a top-of-the-line Ford or Plymouth. Almost certainly a full-size American car anyway.

The one recovered paint chip was brown. There were three fragments of a headlight. Eventually the lab would be able, from the paint chip and the headlight fragments, to tell us the make and model and maybe even the year of the death car, but I didn't know whether our lab could do that or whether the evidence would have to go to Austin or maybe even to Washington.

I don't remember exactly what I told the reporters. Basically I told them we had—as they'd guessed—a murder-for-profit scheme going on. It involved kidnapping and it involved murder, and the one possible witness we'd been trying to find had just been found dead. So had two other people who hadn't really been witnesses at all.

"Detective Ralston," one of them asked, "is the FBI involved in this investigation?"

Everybody loves the FBI sometimes. "Yes."

"Do you feel you're about to close in on those responsible?"

"Not yet."

"What are you doing about it?"

"I can't give you details of our investigation at this time."

"So what you're saying is that while the Fort Worth Police Department and the FBI are sitting around on their duff, women are being murdered?"

"You said that; I didn't."

"Then what are *you* saying?"

"That an investigation is in progress and I'm not going to risk compromising that investigation by telling you exactly what we're doing. I can tell you there are people in this city who have bought babies from this ring, and none of this would be happening if the criminals didn't have a market. I can tell you that there are people in this city who could pick up the telephone and call me and tell me who the criminals are. There are people in this city—respected citizens—who know. But they've got an unspoken conspiracy not to tell me. In some cases it's because they want what they want and they don't care who has to suffer, who has to die, for them to get it. In other cases it's because they are so utterly terrified of what would happen to them, or to babies they dearly love, that they won't call even though they know they should. Some of them have convinced themselves the situation isn't what it is. Some of them are willfully shutting their eyes to the truth, and some of them honestly don't know. They've let themselves believe that what they did was really okay, it's just that the law is nit-picking. I've talked to some of these people, and some of them I'm really sorry for. None of them have told me what they know I have to know. I can't force them to tell me anything. By law, I can't force them to talk to me; I can't even force them to *listen* to me until I can prove what I've said, and so far I can't."

"Are you saying that all private adoptions are immoral?" asked one reporter.

"Certainly not. But I am saying there's a lot of difference between paying the doctor and hospital bills of some nineteen-year-old who's asked her doctor to help her find somebody to adopt her baby, and handing over ten or twelve thousand dollars to somebody to buy a baby. And the difference is this: When you've got a good, decent, respectable doctor, and a good, decent, respectable lawyer involved, chances are the natural mother knows what she's doing and has made a reasonably informed decision. Even then things can go wrong. But paying cash to buy a baby—look, we've all seen the newspapers, babies kidnapped from women in Mexico to be sold to prospective adoptive parents in the United States. That's horrible—and it's happening in the United States too, that babies are kidnapped to be sold. And in some cases—apparently in this case—the natural mothers are being murdered."

"Is that a fact, or is it just your opinion?" a television reporter asked me. Video cameras were running.

"I can't yet go into court and swear to it as a fact," I said, "so I guess at this point it's legally an opinion. But it's backed up by fact, as you can tell if you'll read your own newspapers and listen to your own investigative reporters. And I can't believe that any woman loving enough to adopt a baby, and give it love, and care, and concern, would really want another woman murdered over that same baby."

"You mentioned the word 'conspiracy.' Did you use it loosely, or is there an actual conspiracy involved?"

"As far as we can tell right now, the women are being kidnapped. That is definitely fact, that pregnant women are being kidnapped from at least two states so far. They're being held at an unknown location until their babies are born, and we have at least one baby definitely located that came from that ring. That means somebody is handling the paperwork, somebody is delivering the babies, somebody is making the arrangements with the people who are taking the babies. That's conspiracy, by the definition of the law. We have reason to believe that the women are being killed after their babies are born. And the people who are buying those babies are agreeing to keep the secret of how they acquired the babies. I call that being involved in a conspiracy. Of course it's an unwitting conspiracy, because the adoptive parents in most of the cases we've looked at so far honestly have no idea the women are being maltreated; they honestly think they're taking babies from a situation where they might be neglected. But I don't know what the DA's office is going to call it once the lid blows off. I know I wouldn't want to be in any of those people's shoes."

One of the reporters said, "You know who's taken some of the babies? Will you give us some names?"

I stared at him, aghast. "Certainly not. Now that's enough questions. I think you'll agree with me that I have work to do."

Captain Millner said, "Clear the case. The hell with overtime. I'll argue with city hall."

Okay. What have I got?

We know they're being held somewhere near Summerfields. That's a kind of funny location, because the 820–I-35 split is building up fast. There's been a rumor for years that IBM is getting ready to build a big plant in that area, and land values have risen accordingly. There are three or four big housing developers working in the area—Fox and Jacobs, U.S. Homes, two or three more— and the big bottling plant, and— Oh, I don't remember, a lot of new manufacturing, and of course Motorola has been there for donkey's years.

But—and here's what makes it funny—it's also still heavily agricultural. Scattered among the new expensive modern developments and the new bank that's within screaming distance of where I found Grace dead, there are still little family farms, truck farms, dairies, egg farms, greenhouses—there are hundreds, maybe thousands, of places that are big enough to hide several kidnapped women, far enough away from everything that nobody could hear them scream, land agricultural enough that newly dug earth would excite no notice at all.

And even if I went and knocked on every door of every known house within ten—even fifteen—miles of my house, there's no reason to assume that I'd find them, because the place could be camouflaged, they could be hidden at a place that is supposedly deserted, somebody's deer-hunting cabin or something like that.

We'd need an army.

What would be the chances of getting help from the National Guard?

I'd hate to think I'd have to teach rules of evidence to the National Guard, and while getting the women back alive that are still alive is the first priority, convicting the criminals is top priority too.

My brain was skipping around like a hoptoad. It went now to the girl dead in the ditch, Grace Hammond as I'd first seen her, with one hand thrust out in mute appeal for help that never came, the other clutching a small tree to brace herself for the blow that killed her.

Why didn't she call the police? If that was Grace that went to the Golden Burger—and I was pretty sure it was—why didn't she call the police? She attempted two telephone calls that didn't go through, but she didn't try to call the police, and when Don Coles offered to take her somewhere, she didn't ask him to take her to the police station that was only a few blocks away. Why?

And why, why, why didn't they bury the body?

Why did they just leave her there, when they had to have a place where they could have buried her? I knew they had such a place because they were burying other people somewhere—they had to be, because they couldn't risk turning the other women loose . . .

My mind was skittish, jumping too rapidly from one idea to another that seemed unrelated. Perhaps I was too tired and too depressed to think as accurately as usual, because all the connections kept evading me, staying tantalizingly just on the edges of my conscious thought. But I was beginning at last to make a connection maybe I should have made sooner.

A big car. It was a big car, a big brown car, that killed Rachel Strada.

A big brown car that didn't have any trim to be left in the middle of the street or on Rachel's body along with paint fragments, along with pieces of a broken headlight.

A woman could have killed Grace, but a woman, unless she was an extremely strong woman, couldn't have lifted the 160-odd pounds of dead weight out of the ditch and thrust her into a car to take her somewhere else and bury her.

A man and a woman both had worked together to try to lure me out of my car, so they could kill—Hal, or me, or both?

A woman had worked with Rachel; that woman could have been not only the second midwife I knew I had to have but also the guard, the one who put food inside—cages—for captives, who kept doors locked so captives wouldn't escape.

And that woman, temporarily off guard because she was delivering another woman's baby, could have been overpowered by a strong, young, desperate woman. And if she was delivering another woman's baby, she'd have had to attend to that and wait and go after Grace later—no, that wouldn't work; she'd have been too afraid of what Grace might say and who she might say it to. She'd have left the woman in labor alone and gone after Grace, unless she'd been knocked unconscious. And if she was knocked unconscious, then she'd have gone looking for Grace as soon as she woke up, even if the man she worked with couldn't be reached . . .

Because he was on duty?

Who could have gotten all these women out of their cars so easily? There was never a sign of a struggle, not once, in Texas or in Oklahoma. The ones out of town, in some cases, had taken their cars with them, but in no case at all had there been a sign of a struggle.

If a cop orders you out of your car, you get out of your car.

Nobody would have noticed a cop in Frank Kirk's yard, a cop at Grace Hammond's door.

Pat barked loud and hard at whoever was in our yard. The only people he normally barks that hard at are people in uniform. That was why Bill was puzzled, because I had told him Pat barks only at people in uniform. And that had told him, as it should have told me, that whoever was in our yard was in uniform.

There are big brown police cars—they are driven by some of the deputy sheriffs, and by some of the deputy constables, and by some of the—detectives. . . ?

If a cop has kidnapped you, and you are pretty sure he's a real cop, and you don't know what department he's from, you wouldn't dare go to a police station for help.

There was a cop in on this.

There had to be.

I called Captain Millner.

· 14 ·

As I HAD EXPECTED, Captain Millner didn't like the theory.

But then I didn't like it much either. Not as a fact. I liked it just fine as an explanation of what had happened. I just didn't like to think a police officer would be involved in that kind of crime. Actually in any kind of crime, but especially the kind I was looking at.

I was going to have a lot of work to do Monday. At last I was firmly on the trail of a theory, but the investigation had to wait until more people were available for interviewing. I'd go home, feed my family, and do a lot of thinking; that way I'd be nice and fresh and ready to tackle the job.

But before going home I had one more little project.

Since Rachel was dead, it couldn't hurt anything for me to search her apartment. I obtained a search warrant with no particular difficulty—after today getting search warrants shouldn't be too hard, as long as I was on this case—and I went out on Rosedale, intending to ask our stakeout to help me search. It is not departmental policy to serve search warrants alone—also, it is somewhat unsafe—and by using the stakeout man I wouldn't be asking anybody else to work overtime.

The stakeout man was on his normal shift.

Ernesto Rubacava was there again. I told him what was going on, and he said, "I wish somebody had thought to tell me."

"I just told you. Come on, I can't kick a door in by myself." Kicking a door in is both an art and a science. It helps if you're six feet tall.

We didn't have to kick the door in. It was unlocked, and when we opened it, Ernesto and I both swore. The place had already been searched, with much more thoroughness than finesse.

We'd had it under surveillance since Friday. It must have been searched before then.

After that I didn't expect to find anything evidentiary.

I didn't. Neither did the lab when I called them out.

Ernesto checked in to see what he should do for the rest of his shift, and I went home.

There isn't any six o'clock news on Sunday, but there were periodic newsbreaks telling people to tune in at ten for an update on the Fort Worth murder-for-profit story. They had quite a lot to say about it on the ten o'clock news, including a videotape of me running my mouth.

My telephone rang at ten forty-five. She didn't give her name. But she didn't need to, because her first words told me who she was. "Mrs. Ralston, was Junie's birth mother killed? Was that what you came to see me about?" She was crying.

"Yes, Irene, it was," I told her.

"Then why didn't you say so then?"

"Because I could see you didn't know a thing about it, and I didn't want to upset you."

"Didn't want to upset me! Look, I don't know what to do. Eddie got real mad when that news story came on and he went and shut himself up in his study and started calling people, and when I asked him what was wrong he called me a bitch and said he should have had better sense than to fall for me, and then he slammed his door and got back on the phone. So I got Junie's diaper bag and sneaked out with her and I walked to 7-Eleven and I don't want to go back home and I don't know what to do."

"Is he likely to guess you're at 7-Eleven?"

"I don't think so. But the pay phones are outside. He could see me, if he drove past looking."

I thought about what 7-Eleven she was likely to be at, and then I asked, to be sure I was thinking of the right one. Good. It had a little alcove where the video games were; it was impossible from the street to see into that alcove. I told her to go in there and wait for me.

It was going to take me over half an hour, probably closer to forty-five minutes, to drive over there. But I was afraid to send a marked car to get her, even though our marked cars aren't brown, because . . .

Some of our marked cars *are* brown. Not very many of them, but some. I had forgotten that.

I told her to hide in there in the alcove by the video games, and if Eddie tried to get her, she was to scream as loud as she could for somebody to call the cops. I told her I'd be there as soon as I could.

She was waiting for me; she came out as I drove up and got into the passengers' side of my car, carrying the baby and a diaper bag and nothing else. Her first words were, "Why didn't you tell me?"

"I just didn't see any need to yet. You'd have known eventually."

"Yeah." She shivered. "He's acting like he's crazy. I never saw anybody acting like he's acting. He's banging things and hollering and saying he wusht he'd never heard of me . . . Look, I knew it wasn't going to be any bag of lollipops being married to an old man, but he begged and he begged and he begged and I finally didn't have the heart to keep on saying no. If I'd known we was going to live like this, I'd have said no anyway. What happens to Junie?"

"Eventually, when we find out who she belongs to, she goes back there."

"And her mama's dead and her papa'll have to work so she'll

have to go to one of those day-care centers. Maybe he'll let me take care of her for him, do you think? Only I can't do that," she said, "because I'll have to get some sort of job. I don't know how I'll do that. Eddie's got all my clothes and stuff and he's not going to want to give them back. I could go back to the farm and run a tractor, I guess, but there's still seven kids at home and there's not much room for me."

Eddie would have to give her clothes back. And Texas law said that half of what was in that house belonged to Irene. Of course the question would be whether she could make that law stick. Eddie had money and she didn't.

Texas law does *not* provide for alimony. Irene was right that she was going to have to get a job. Although come to think of it that wasn't altogether certain either—Texas is a community property state. And the house at least hinted around that Eddie might have quite a lot of money.

"Why are we stopping here?" Irene asked.

"A friend of mine lives here. I'm going to borrow a playpen for Junie to sleep in."

Olead, yawning and politely pointing out that he had an exam in the morning, got the playpen and pad out of his shed and helped me stick them in my trunk.

The stakeout car was still waiting by my house. This time it was brown.

I was definitely getting paranoid.

I looked to see who was in the brown car. It was David Conners; he was sprawled out in the front seat reading by flashlight and listening to a small tape recorder.

He was reading the Bible and listening to a tape of the Mormon Tabernacle Choir.

Somehow I did not think it was David Conner who deliberately ran over Rachel Strada last night in front of the Greyhound Bus Station.

He looked up and said, "Hi, Deb. Everything's all nice and quiet, and I think your pup is getting to like me."

"Good. I hope you guys can be pulled off this soon."

"I kinda hope so myself," he said candidly. "This is a drag."

Hal and Becky were asleep; Harry had waited up for me. He was sitting at the radio table talking to somebody in Japan. I introduced Irene and he greeted her, turned off the radio, and announced he was going to bed.

Irene and I sat in the living room and talked for a little while, but she didn't really have anything to add to what she'd already said. She didn't know what kind of work Eddie did, she didn't know where he worked, and she didn't know how much money he had. Since we talked, she'd tried again to find out, but Eddie had just called her a snoopy bitch.

They'd only been married for six months. He'd been a real lover boy the first month, and after that it was like she wasn't there except to cook and clean, and, well, you know. She guessed he'd gotten the baby to shut her up, like you'd buy a little girl a doll.

I wondered why he'd bothered; it didn't seem to be in character for Eddie. But maybe he'd figured it would keep Irene from nagging at him.

One more little thing emerged, but it wasn't worth much: Irene had gone with him to pick up the baby. She knew they'd gone north and then a little ways east on Loop 820, but she didn't remember what exit they'd taken off Loop 820. They'd gone north off Loop 820, though; Irene was a farm girl and she knew north from south, and besides that it was right at sunset when anybody'd know. They'd gone north a ways and then they'd turned left, which of course was west, and they'd turned again only she didn't remember which way—oh, yes, it was right, and then left again into a field and there were some right good-looking heifers in one of the fields they'd passed.

The house was old and painted white, and there were hedges around the side of it so she couldn't see behind it. Eddie had told her to stay in the car and he'd gone in and come back out with the baby, and all she was wearing was a disposable diaper and she was all wrapped up in a scratchy old blanket, but that was okay because Irene had brought the diaper bag with her and she had a little pink dress for her and they took her home in the little pink dress.

Irene guessed she would like to go to sleep now, so I got her one of my nightgowns.

Later in the night I heard her crying. I didn't go to check on her because she hadn't cried in front of me; that told me she needed to be alone to cry.

Harry had taken the week off to look after the house, before the stakeout showed up. He wasn't going to change his mind, he said, because if other things got too sticky, the stakeout might have to be withdrawn and sent somewhere else.

Irene said she needed to start thinking about somewhere to go. I told her I would suggest she stay exactly where she was for now; we had room for her at least for a few days, and I wanted to be sure she was safe.

Harry delivered Hal to school as he had done on Friday. Today I didn't think I was going to feel a compulsion to call every hour or so to be sure he was safe. I was sure by now that they had been after me, not Hal.

I wanted to talk with Dutch, but he was off somewhere.

There were more Teletypes on my desk. Ardmore, Oklahoma, was missing Jeanette Munning as of September 11; her baby was due October 5. Durant, Oklahoma, was missing Ginger Zimmerman; she'd gone missing September 18 and her baby was due September 30.

I knew we had a high murder rate in Fort Worth—eleventh in the country now, ahead of both Los Angeles and New York— but importing women in order to kill them was pushing it a little.

Of course Ginger might be alive. Jeanette almost certainly was.

There were things I needed to check on. I started making a list.

Like: Who, and what, was Eddie O'Neal? He wasn't a gangster because if he was I'd have heard of him, but from what Irene told me, he was acting like one.

Like: A complete rundown of exactly when each of the women had been kidnapped. If I was right that there was only one man working directly with the ring, and that man was some kind of law enforcement officer, then the Fort Worth victims had to have been kidnapped when he was off duty. He wouldn't dare risk getting a sudden call with a kidnap victim in his police car.

The out-of-town ones—at least the ones farther away than the immediate metroplex area—almost certainly had to have been kidnapped on his day off.

He had to be off duty when he went after me.

He almost certainly was *on* duty when he got Rachel Strada. From the times everything had been happening, I was guessing he was on morning watch—midnight till 8 A.M. I checked the time Rachel Strada was killed. Yes, I was right—it was almost one in the morning.

But if he worked morning watch, why wasn't he available when Grace got away?

Was he in court?

I needed to check all the police agencies in the area and find out if any of their cars had reported accidents the night of the hit-and-run, because he was going to have to come up with some kind of explanation for the broken headlight, the chipped paint.

If it was me, I'd have first run the car through a car wash to get rid of as much as possible of the blood, hair, tissue, fiber, from hitting Rachel Strada, and then I'd stage an accident. And this man wasn't any less smart than me. In fact, I was beginning to be afraid he was smarter than me.

"Hi, Deb," said Special Agent William T. Arnold.

"Hi, Dub," I said vaguely, and went on thinking.

"Deb," he said, "it has been brought to my attention, both by your boss and by my boss, that Deb and Dub are doing the Tweedledum and Tweedledee act again, by which I mean that we seem to be working together. So would you mind letting me in on what we're doing?"

"Oh, yeah," I said, "what did you find out on Patten?"

"Not a whole heck of a lot," he said, "except that he's been spending a lot more money than he can reasonably account for having. Either he's got a great big legacy or he's robbed a bank, only none of his relatives have died and we haven't had any big bank robberies lately. We're still checking background, but all we've got so far is, he went in the Army right from high school and then he got out of the Army and went to work in that meat-packing plant. Now what've you got?"

I handed him reports, notes, and started making a written list of the things he could check on easier than I could. "Okay," he said, "I'll find out about these police car wrecks first thing."

"Okay," I said, "and I'll start visiting midwives."

I didn't seem to have a task force any longer. They had finished their task of computer entry and gone back on patrol. But maybe, just maybe, I didn't need one any longer.

"Before we do either one of those," Dub suggested, "let's have a look at the lay of the land. Let's see, she turned north off Loop 820, west off that road, north again, then west, only that one was onto a farm. Okay, let's see what the map looks like."

Most likely she'd have turned north onto Beach Street, Denton Highway, or Rufe Snow Drive—she wasn't familiar enough with the area to have remembered landmarks, and of course she hadn't really been paying any attention anyhow.

From there, there were umpteen places to turn in any of the directions she'd given us. Somebody was going to have to go and take every one of the possibles and see if it looked like the description.

I asked Captain Millner if he could get me some patrolmen again, and he said he felt quite sure he could do that.

I wrote the directions down and asked him to instruct them to get out there, out of uniform, not in marked cars, and start driving, taking every possible road that could fit those very vague instructions until they found a place that could fit the description, and then report in.

"Deb," he said, "you do know that almost all of these places are outside of our jurisdiction, don't you?"

"Well, yeah, but . . ."

He sat down with the Mapsco. "We need," he said, "to get a local officer from each of those jurisdictions involved."

"Captain Millner," I said, "we can't. Not yet. Not until I know—"

He turned and looked at me. "A sheriff's man then?"

"Captain Millner, they drive brown cars. The sheriff's department drives brown cars."

"Oh, yeah," he said. "Well, there is that to think about. Okay. I guess, since they won't be doing anything but looking . . ."

I had narrowed it down to a list of ten midwives. Pauline Baxter, Annie Pooley, Abby Kingston, Stephanie Carter, Darla Miller, Nickie White, Edith Shuman, Gladys Buttrey, Beverly Majors, Hazel Anderson.

I hadn't asked for race on my printout, which was a mistake. But I still had the stack of original paperwork my "task force" had worked from.

It availed me nothing—unincorporated Tarrant County was on a computer, and what I had from that office was a computer tape. I didn't have paper printouts, and it would take time to write another program. More time than I felt I had right now.

I picked up my notebook and went over to the courthouse, which is now much closer than it was before our new building was built, to start looking up actual birth certificates. Luckily birth records are still a matter of public record; the women in the county clerk's office showed me where the books were and left me alone.

The babies delivered by Pauline Baxter were all white. So were the babies delivered by Darla Miller, Edith Shuman, Gladys Buttrey, and Beverly Majors. The babies delivered by Annie Pooley, Abby Kingston, Stephanie Carter, Nickie White, and Hazel Anderson were nearly all black. So, presumably, were Annie Pooley, Abby Kingston, Stephanie Carter, Nickie White, and Hazel Anderson.

Pauline Baxter had her own listing in the phone book, with a neat little "mdwf" beside it. So did Darla Miller. Edith Shuman, Gladys Buttrey, and Beverly Majors didn't.

On the other hand, there was no reason to assume the woman delivering babies to be sold was not also a legitimate midwife.

Calling them in my own persona might not be such a good idea right now. But I am a woman. And a woman can be pregnant and hunting a midwife. I took the phone into an interview room so that there would be absolutely, positively, no police noise in the background, especially in view of the fact that if I was right the woman I was looking for would be familiar with the sound of a telephone with police noise in the background.

My name is Debra Lynn Ralston. I didn't dare be Deb Ralston. But my maiden name was Gordon. I'd be Lynn Gordon.

Just in time I realized—I couldn't do this. They weren't all listed in the yellow pages; the phone book wasn't all that out of date, but even so, three of these women hadn't made it. You'd have to hear about them by word of mouth, or you'd never find them. And I didn't have any convincing explanation of how I had heard about them—"Somebody told me in the laundromat" wouldn't work if the woman I was looking for had no legitimate business.

No, I'd better wait and put those names together with whatever Dub got, and if we came up with a name that matched, well, then we'd be in business.

I called Records and asked if they had any record on Edward O'Neal. I gave address and age and told them I didn't know date of birth; Irene hadn't been able to remember.

Records did not have anything on Edward O'Neal.

I should have thought to hand that over to Dub.

I called the local FBI office and asked the agent who answered to have Dub see what he could turn up on Edward

O'Neal, and the agent I was talking with answered, "Don't you know who that is?"

"No, should I?"

"Well, I don't guess there's any reason why you should. But they ran him out of Vegas a coupla years ago when he got caught running a crooked roulette wheel; you know the gaming boards in Nevada are very strict with that kind of thing. He lost his casino license, and then right after that his name came up in a racketeering probe. He sort of, like I said, left Vegas. Turned up in Atlantic City for a while, but he couldn't get a license there either, and—he's not mixed up in your case, is he?"

"Obviously he is. At least if it's the same Edward O'Neal."

"Well, well, well," the agent said. "I'm going to walk over and talk with your intelligence section."

When we were in the old building, it took about three minutes for an FBI agent to walk over to the police station. Or vice versa, of course. It now takes about fifteen. That is one of the penalities we paid for getting a new building.

In exactly seventeen minutes Ron Elgart from Intelligence banged into our office, corralled Captain Millner, and slammed the door in my face.

A little bit after that Captain Millner opened the door and beckoned me into the interview room. "Now tell Deb what you told me," he said.

Elgart swallowed. "It's a metro intelligence case," he said. "If word gets out—"

"Word won't get out. Deb has a need to know."

"O'Neal's running a gambling operation. We're getting ready to shut it down. It advertises by word of mouth, and it's probably got protection in the jurisdiction it's in, but that's not for certain—we're not telling them until the last minute, just in case. It's big. It's a Vegas-style operation, only I think the odds are sort of fixed in the direction of the house. All kinds of gambling—roulette, poker, blackjack, dice, you name it, and plenty of booze and pretty girls to keep the marks' minds off what they're doing. I don't want him spooked."

"I expect," I told him, "that protecting his gambling operation is toward the low end of his conscious mind right now. He's fixing to be dropped on for a black market baby, and he knows it."

"And if he's dropped on for anything, everything'll come out. You some kind of dumb-ass, Deb? We better move on in—I've got to get on the phone."

He took off again.

Mr. Eddie O'Neal was explained. All except how he had made contact with the baby merchants.

·15·

Dub was back. That hadn't taken long, but of course he'd gotten his information on the telephone. It helps to be an FBI agent. People are afraid to ignore you.

There'd been three police car wrecks in the Fort Worth metroplex area that night. A Fort Worth patrol car, black and white, had collided with another car during a high-speed chase of a drunk driver. About ten witnesses. Driver's name: Dean Lewis.

A Watauga police car, pale blue, backed into a tree while leaving the scene of a burglary with his headlights off because he had the burglar in sight. No witnesses except of course the burglar. Driver's name: Frank Heyden.

A deputy constable car, light brown, skidded off the road on loose sand and hit a tree. It was still in the shop. No witnesses. Driver's name: Doyle Bernard.

None of those names matched the names of any of the midwives. I'd been rather assuming a husband-and-wife partnership, but of course that wasn't in any way necessary.

A black and white patrol car or a light blue patrol car hadn't left the brown paint chips near Rachel Strada's body. A brown deputy constable car might have, but it would take a lab, not me, to find out.

"Let's just go over and have a look at that brown one," I suggested to Dub, and he said, "I was wondering when you were going to ask."

We went to the garage where the county cars are repaired. It wasn't hard to find the deputy constable car. It had a constable's insignia painted on the side, overpainted with the specific constable's name, and it had electioneering bumper stickers all over the front and rear bumpers. Constables' cars tend to be like that.

It had certainly hit a tree; there were mesquite leaves caught in one of the cracks. But that was no proof that it hadn't hit something else before it hit the tree. There was extensive damage to the left front headlight and the grille, as well as to the fender on the left.

Dub asked the repairman, "Do you mind if I take some paint and glass samples?"

"Don't know what you want them for, but you're welcome to them. I'm going to have to rebuild the whole damn front end."

"You heard that," Dub said to me, and I agreed with him that I had heard that.

He had coin envelopes in his pocket. He dug them and his pocketknife out, and he flicked off samples of the paint and nudged them into the first envelope. He wrote on it, "Paint samples from left front fender, 1985 Ford—" He wrote down the vehicle identification number from the inspection sticker, and handed it to me. I initialed and dated it too, as he bent over again to collect fragments of the glass from the headlight. That second envelope was similarly labeled, and as we strolled back out to our cars, I asked, "Dub, what good is that going to do you? Our accident investigators have the glass and paint from the scene."

"Right now they do," he said blandly.

RHIP. Rank Has Its Privileges. Or, in the case of the FBI, Rank Has Its Clout.

But like it or not, it takes a while to get a report back from the

FBI laboratory, and that was time that could cost lives. We didn't have time to wait.

There are a thousand avenues to take, if you have time for a leisurely investigation. But every hour we waited might mean another death, and as Dub and I drove back to the police station, each of us was thinking of ways we could proceed that would get the whole thing over with *fast*. "I'm going to check on something," Dub told me. "I'll be back later." I dropped him by the Federal Building.

In my office Dutch Van Flagg, looking very pleased with himself, was on the phone to the district attorney's office about a search warrant. Apparently he now had a very good idea who had bombed the clinic. I wasn't paying a lot of attention until I heard him spelling the name. "P-a-t-t-e-n," he said. "Not o-n, e-n. Be sure of that. Nicholas. Yes, Nicholas Timothy. Got it? When? Okay, I'll pick it up." He hung up. "Warrant'll be ready at two o'clock. You want to go with me, Deb?"

"What are we searching him for? The shootings? I thought it was the bombing you were talking about."

"It was."

"But what has he got to do with—"

"Ours not to reason why and so forth," Dutch said. "I got on him bass-ackwards actually."

"Meaning?"

"You know all those magazines I was looking at Saturday?"

"Yeah, I looked at some of them Sunday," I said. "I saw the ads, but . . ."

Dutch leaned back in his chair and struck a very professorial pose. "To start with, before your case and mine intersected, I was looking at one of those militant so-called Christian organizations, you know, the kind that hates the Jews and the Catholics and the Mormons and is pretty sure all good Christians are white? Some of their officers had written letters to the *Startlegram* promising to blow up the clinics if they weren't closed. The paper didn't print any of the letters, of course, but they did keep us posted, and I picked up all the letters."

"The *Startlegram*" is an old nickname for the *Fort Worth Star-Telegram,* and I remembered seeing Dutch with the stack of letters.

"When I went over to search, they told me they hadn't actually *done* anything yet, and they didn't seem worried, but I still searched the organizational headquarters and the homes of all the officers. I didn't find anything that could have been used to make a bomb, but I did see copies of this magazine with the ad circled. Well, I really didn't have any probable cause to seize the magazine, but I went out and bought a copy of it for myself and then got the postal inspectors involved. Their classified editor was real cooperative," he added, "once the postal inspector got it across to them they could be shut down for knowingly aiding a terrorist organization. So then I found out the ad was inserted by Mr. Nicholas Timothy Patten, and we checked a fingerprint from one of the firebombs against his Army record and it matched right up. Of course now I've got to find out who hired him, but you know what? I'll bet he'll tell me. Anyhow, you want to go with me?"

I wasn't that sure Nick Patten would tell anybody anything. "You need me?" I asked.

"Uh-uh. It's in Arlington, so I've got to get some Arlington people to go along, and that ought to be enough."

"Good, because I've got something else to do. Dutch," I added, "what about the letter?"

"The letter."

"The letter. That Grace was supposed to have sent Dr. Kirk. That I thought you were checking on this morning. That letter."

"That letter," he said, "is no more."

"Yeah?"

"Mrs. Kirk said the mail went to a post office box and the receptionist picked it up. She told me how to reach the receptionist. The receptionist told me she went about three o'clock to pick up the mail, the day of—well, actually the day *before* the bombing, since it was after midnight."

"I know when the bombing was."

"So there was a letter there from Grace. She said she remembered the name because the girl kept canceling appointments. So she put the letter on the doctor's desk. And the doctor was busy all the rest of the afternoon and never got to his mail. She reminded him of it and he told her he'd get to it tomorrow."

Five people had died for that letter. And it didn't even exist. "Shit," I said, and Dutch said, "Yeah."

So everything was at least beginning to click together. Nick and Jackie bought a baby—Jackie told Grace about it—Grace wanted to sell a baby. Yes, if they knew of Nick's expertise, Nick would certainly be the appropriate one to bomb the clinic. And they'd probably have refunded his money, maybe even have paid him a little more; that was how he got out of Sherman—but now?

They couldn't blackmail Nick, not anymore, because Nick had as much on them as they had on him, but Nick had good reason to help them keep the secrets. If the house of cards fell, it all fell together.

Only I didn't think Nick was going to tell everything he knew. Or anything he knew. I figured Nick would bluff as long as he thought he had one card left in his hand.

I didn't know what Dub had gone to check on. I had armies of men—well, at least I had three men—out checking roads in northeast Tarrant County. But damn it . . .

"Captain," I said, "I've got an idea. I'm going in my personal car. But I'll stay on the radio."

Actually it wasn't my personal car; it was a rental car, because my personal car was still being fixed. But that was all the better. If I was lucky, it might not have been spotted as mine yet.

I went home.

Irene was sitting on the couch talking to the baby, who was cooing, and Harry was fiddling with diagrams for a linear amplifier he was going to be building one of these days when he got around to it.

"Harry," I asked, "do you mind baby-sitting?"

"Uh-uh, glad to," he said. "Why?"

"Irene," I said, "you want to help me?"

"Can I?"

"I hope so."

We went south on Beach Street and turned right on Great Western Parkway—I finally remembered the name—and turned south on 35 and went back around to Loop 820. Now I had us on the highway Eddie had taken her on. "Tell me if it looks right," I said.

I took the Beach Street exit. "This is the way to your house," Irene said.

"Yes. But is it the way you and Eddie went to get the baby? Think hard. Try to be sure, but tell me even if you're not sure, if you have a good idea."

"It's not," she said. "We didn't come this way. There were a lot of stores and stuff, not cow pastures and things like that."

"Fine."

That eliminated one possibility. I went back up Beach Street and turned right as I had done before, looping back around to 820 again; I was sticking to that route because I wanted to avoid creating familiarity with any other route while Irene was trying to remember. This time I exited on Denton Highway.

Now I had stores—a restaurant, a gasoline station, a grocery store, a big lumber store. I glanced at Irene. She was looking worried. "No," she said. "I just remembered. There was a McDonald's. There was a McDonald's we passed; I remember that."

"Now we're cooking," I told her. "Rufe Snow."

We swung on over to Rufe Snow. There was her McDonald's. There was her shopping center. Out of the corner of my eye I saw her face. This was the right road, and she was sure of it. "What next?" I asked. "You said we turn to the west next."

"I don't know. I don't know the names of any of the streets."

"I don't know the names of the streets out here either, Irene,"

I told her. "Don't worry about that. That's what I've got a Mapsco for. All you've got to do is show me where the street is."

"I hope I'll recognize it. Just keep going."

We kept going. After a while I said, "Irene?"

"Still keep going."

"We're about to run out of road."

She was silent for a moment. Then she said, "That's it! We did run out of road. This road ends into another one and that was where we went west."

"Okay." I pulled over to the side of the street and opened the Mapsco. I'd driven, in the past, on the road she was talking about, but I didn't have the slightest idea what it was called.

The map said it was called Bursey Road.

We turned west on Bursey Road and kept going. And kept going. When we crossed Denton Highway, I was afraid we'd gone too far—why would he have gone this way, when he could have just turned down Denton Highway to start with? But Irene said, "Keep going."

It wasn't Bursey Road anymore. Now it was Wall Price Road.

We finally turned north onto Ray White Road, and a while after that we turned left onto a gravel and clay track.

Which seemed to run exactly nowhere at all, except into a maze of mesquite trees so thick I was afraid one of the thorns was going to puncture a tire. But Irene had relaxed. "This is it," she said.

We came out of the maze of mesquite trees into a field. Ahead of me was a two-story white frame house with, not a hedge, but an overgrown trellised wall on both sides of it, so that it was impossible to see beyond the house.

There was a brown car parked in front of the house. It had MAJORS SECURITY SERVICE painted on the side, and a badge.

Security guards. I'd been a fool not to think of that. And of course at night a woman, probably used even in this age of liberation to passive obedience, wasn't going to distinguish between a security guard uniform and a police uniform.

Pat couldn't either. In fact he couldn't, as I was well aware, distinguish between a mail carrier's uniform and a police uniform.

"Irene," I said, "could you find the way here again?"

"Sure."

"Remember where we crossed Denton Highway? That's going to be the closest telephone. Go back there and dial 911. Tell whoever answers that a Fort Worth police officer needs help. Give them your location, and tell them you'll meet them at that telephone and lead them to the scene. And tell them to hurry!"

"But Deb—"

"Do as I tell you!"

I was only going to keep an eye on things, of course, because it wasn't inside the city limits of Fort Worth and I had no more authority there than any private citizen. But at least I could make sure nobody got killed in the next hour. I got out of the car, and she slid over into the driver's seat and turned the car around. I was alone, with a .38 revolver with six rounds of ammo in it I didn't expect to need, and a dead radio I was just fixing to put down because it was encumbering my hands.

The background around here was all green and brown. Cammies would work very well.

I was wearing black slacks and a red blouse and black canvas sandals.

Have you ever tried to hide in a mesquite thicket in sandals?

Or in anything else, for that matter. Mesquite trees were undoubtedly invented by the devil—they have beautiful lacy leaves to entice you and three-inch thorns to impale you with as soon as you've been lured into their clutches.

And somewhere I could hear a woman screaming.

I headed in that direction, and a man behind me said, "Where do you think you're going?"

I whirled.

He had a shotgun.

▫ 16 ▫

Mɪss Mᴀɴɴᴇʀs ʜᴀs ɢɪᴠᴇɴ no instructions on how a lady should greet a gentleman who happens to be pointing a shotgun at her.

And I didn't have any pointers to give her.

I was pretty sure my mouth was hanging open, and I frankly hadn't the faintest idea what I was going to do next. My general rule on what to do when faced with a shotgun—which I'd never had to implement, because I'd never been on the north end of a northbound shotgun before—is to do what the person on the other end of it says, and so far this man hadn't told me anything to do. He'd just asked a question.

He asked it again. "Where do you think you're going?"

"There's somebody over there screaming," I pointed out.

"That doesn't answer the question."

"Well, I thought maybe I'd better go see why she's screaming."

"She's screaming because she's having a baby and she doesn't seem to be too happy about it."

"Then maybe we'd better get her a doctor." I headed enthusiastically toward the house. He motioned the shotgun at me suggestively and I stopped.

"She's got somebody with her. Now I'm asking again. What are you doing here?"

I shrugged. "Looking for you, of course. It was pretty crappy of you to shoot at my son."

"Your son? You mean there was a kid in the car? I sure as hell didn't see him."

And that settled that question. It was interesting that he hadn't bothered to deny shooting at my car.

But then he probably didn't see any need to deny anything. He didn't plan on my being around long enough to repeat the conversation.

"I suppose you think you're safe," I said. "Well, you're not. You haven't asked how I got here yet."

"I don't need to. You don't think your friend is going anywhere, do you? Turn around and look."

I did.

The rental car was stopped just at the edge of the field; its way was blocked by another brown car.

This one, I could see even at this distance, had damage to the left front fender and headlight area.

"You have been very, very stupid, Deb Ralston," the man said conversationally. "You got in our way. Too bad. You were a pretty nice lady in a lot of ways."

"We've got several officers in unmarked cars prowling around in this area," I said. "They're all trying to find this place. It just happened that Irene and I found it first. But when you fire off that shotgun, they're sure to hear it."

"Not unless they're real, real close."

"That's true. But do you want to take the chance that they're not?"

"No, maybe not," he agreed. "But I will if I have to. Take the pistol out of the holster and drop it on the ground."

As I've said, my rule when faced with a shotgun is to do exactly as I'm told. But I noticed where the pistol fell. I wasn't through yet.

"Now march," he told me.

Through an oval gate in the trellis into a backyard, where a row of what from the air had looked like chicken coops were securely locked and barred. It was from the inside of one of them that the screaming was coming.

He stopped by one that was unlocked. "There's a shovel inside," he said. "Get it."

I got it.

We went on down to a farm pond. He stopped me at the soft earth on its bank. "Now dig," he said.

"Isn't this a little corny?" I asked him.

"Just efficient. I need a couple of graves dug. But I don't want to get dirty; I'm going to work after a while, because we're about to have a vacant—suite. But what difference does it make to you if you get dirty? You're fixing to be dead anyway."

The dirt was soft and moist, and it didn't take me nearly as long as I would have liked it to take me to dig two sizable holes. I could see, nearby, other mounds of earth—twelve of them. More than I'd expected. Apparently some women had never been reported missing, or some towns had never replied to my Teletypes.

Really, it was surprising that my brain was functioning as normally as it was. But apparently some part of me had decided I didn't have time to panic now. After it was all over, then I would panic. But if I wanted to have time to panic later, I'd have to think now.

He told me to put the shovel down.

Then he put his shotgun down, and he headed for me with a knife about the size of the one Rambo used in the movie. I stepped to one side. And I vomited.

Deliberately.

On his arm.

It was remarkably easy to do.

Very few people can resist the reflex to get out of the way when somebody vomits on them. He couldn't. I'd counted on that, and while he was jumping out of the way, I frantically remembered what I could of those self-defense lessons I took so many years ago at Harry's insistence. I'd told him then I didn't ever want to need to use them.

And I hadn't. Until now.

You don't go for a man's crotch, as most self-defense manuals tell you, because he's expecting that and he'll automatically defend it.

If you're wearing spike heels, you come down hard on his foot. But I was wearing sandals with foam soles.

So I did what was left, and it wasn't a trick I'd learned in a class. I went for his nose, and I hit his nose just above his lip with the heel of my hand and drove it back as hard into his head as I could shove, and he dropped at my feet and I checked his pulse and he didn't have one. He didn't have one because that one little maneuver a Secret Service agent had taught me years ago had driven bone fragments from his nose back into his brain.

Feeling unaccountably numb, I rinsed my hands in the farm pond and picked up his shotgun and checked to be sure it was loaded, and then I checked his pockets, got out his car keys, and walked back around to the front of his house and got in his car and drove toward the front end of the driveway, where the other car was still sitting, its driver standing with a shotgun, guarding Irene and waiting for orders.

I got out of the car and he saw me and realized I wasn't the person he'd expected, and he raised the shotgun toward me and I raised the one I was holding and fired, and he spun back against his car, spraying blood and screaming twice but only twice.

I'd never fired a gun before except on the firing range. I'd never needed to.

My theory had always been that usually you don't have to fire, not if you wait for a backup, and have command presence, and use your head.

But this time waiting for a backup didn't work because the person who was going for the backup couldn't get there. And having command presence didn't do a bit of good when the other person had a shotgun.

But I guessed I'd used my head.

At least I was still alive, and so was Irene.

"You okay?" I asked her, and she nodded. "Then go and get help like I told you to," I said, and she nodded again and started the car, to back expertly around the corpse and head back down the driveway toward the road.

The woman I'd heard before was screaming again. I went back toward the house, back through the gap in the hedge, and back toward the row of chicken coops with locks and bars. The door of one of them was standing open. I went inside.

The standing woman must have been about my age, and I recognized her at once. I was surprised I could, because last time I saw her it was nearly full dark, she had smeared makeup and her hair was in her eyes, and I didn't think she was much past twenty. Now she was dressed in slacks and a T-shirt and wearing no makeup, and she was watching as the other woman, the one who was manacled to the table, screamed. She wasn't doing anything, she wasn't saying anything; she was just watching. But she was watching closely. She saw when the other woman's eyes caught sight of me, and she turned.

"What the—" she began, and I clipped her neatly under the chin. I didn't have time to argue, and my handcuffs were in my purse, which was in the car Irene was driving.

"Where's the key?" I asked the woman on the table, and she said, "Her bra. She kept it—" She screamed again. I could see her abdomen rising with another contraction.

I unlocked the chains and the handcuffs, and she turned over on her side and stopped screaming. I started timing.

Three minutes apart. She might yet have time to make it to a hospital, if Irene hurried and if the police she called hurried too.

"I'm Deb Ralston," I told her between contractions. "I'm a Fort Worth police officer. You're safe now—what's your name?"

She told me she was Joanna Ross.

"But your baby was due weeks ago," I said stupidly. And then I started crying.

But not for long, because I had to stop to deliver a baby. It was a novel experience. Not only was Phillip Ross going to have his wife back, he also had a new baby son he was going to be very pleased to meet.

Joanna Ross had become a lot happier about having a baby once she knew she was keeping it.

"There's not much more use lying, is there?" Nick Patten said.

"No," Dutch told him flatly.

He shrugged. "Listen, don't blame Jackie, because she didn't know anything about any of it. All she knew was, I promised her a baby and I got her a baby. Except later, I had to tell her later, but she didn't know until after. And I didn't mean any of this to happen. All I wanted—all Jackie and I wanted—was that baby. There aren't many now, and the regular adoption agencies kept saying we were too young, or our income wasn't good enough, or Jackie was too nervous—that kind of thing. Then— I knew Don Majors in the Army. He told us his wife Bev was a midwife. He could get us a baby, but it would cost. Expenses, he said. Doctors. And lawyers. And there were people he had to pay off. What the hell, it sounded okay. Don's got connections. All kinds of connections. That's the kind of guy Don is."

"Was."

"What?"

"Was. Not Don is. Don was. Donald Majors is past tense."

Donald Majors had been the first man I'd killed. He'd been running a security guard service for years, and he'd been losing money because the market was highly competitive and he'd lost contracts because several buildings he was guarding were burglarized. His checkbook also showed some large checks to Eddie O'Neal, and stuck into it was a torn-up IOU for two thousand dollars from him to O'Neal. We surmised Irene had gotten her baby in partial settlement of a gambling debt—not that we'd ever be able to prove it.

The midwife, Beverly Majors, was Donald's wife. She ran another business on the side; it was called Adoption Counseling.

According to its ad in the yellow pages, it counseled people on what they should do to make themselves more attractive to adoption agencies. It also provided information on how to get in touch with adoption agencies in different states and with foreign agencies, as well as on how to handle private adoptions in Texas. Which would have been a terrific service if it had been legitimate.

The other dead man was Elliot Majors, Donald's younger brother. From what we could tell, mostly he just took orders.

Nick was still talking. "I was really broke after coming up with all that money, and so I got the idea of placing that ad."

"You were expecting legitimate business?" Dutch asked dryly.

Nick half grinned at him. "I was expecting foreign business. Nicaragua, that kind of thing. *Se habla español.* Or *me hablo español,* or something. No, I don't know. Anyhow the ad doesn't matter because Don didn't answer the ad. I told you. Don knew me. *Then* he told me a lot. And I swear to you, that was the first I knew about any kidnappings."

"And Don told you to leave Sherman?"

"No, I decided that. Once I knew—they told me Grace was dead. They said it was an accident; they said they'd have let her go after the baby was born, but she tried to run away and—they said it was an accident. I thought maybe if we moved then, Jackie wouldn't find out. And—I told Don I'd bomb the building if it was empty. He told me it was empty. The son of a bitch told me the building was empty."

And that was when Nick Patten started crying. "The son of a bitch told me the building was empty. I didn't go to *kill* anybody."

It was very convincing, but I wasn't buying any. "Nick," I said softly, "you moved to Arlington *before* Grace died."

He stopped crying and stared at me.

So we had Nick Patten, and we had the surviving members of the gang, and I still didn't feel very happy. I didn't go to kill anybody either.

And there were those babies, those babies who'd been deprived of one mother at birth and now were to lose a second mother so early, so young . . .

The women from Lawton and the women from Ardmore and Durant were alive, and so were two of the women from Texas besides Joanna Ross, and three women from Kansas we hadn't even known about. But there were not twelve, but fifteen filled graves there beside the farm pond, as well as the two that were staying empty.

When Captain Millner finally said I could go home, I went to bed and cried for a long time, and vomited over and over until Harry told me if I didn't go to the doctor he'd wring my neck.

We were still sorting paperwork two days later when I was called to the phone. "Deb? Are you busy?"

"Hello, Irene. No, I'm not busy." I was, of course, but Irene needed somebody to talk to.

"Guess what?"

"I don't know what. Tell me."

"Junie's birth mother was only fifteen and her parents don't want the baby. They say they're too old to raise her. So if I'll agree to let them stay in touch with her and let her know they're her grandparents, they'll let me keep her. And my lawyer said there won't be any problem with the paperwork, since they've consented. Isn't that wonderful?"

It was the best news I had heard in a very long time. I told her so.

"And I'm getting divorced from Eddie, and my lawyers say I get half of everything he has, and Deb, Deb, he has nearly two hundred thousand dollars! So I'll be able to take good care of Junie!"

Two hundred thousand dollars of illegal gambling money. But that wasn't Irene O'Neal's fault, and I was glad some of it was going to help the baby. I hung up the phone. "Cap," I said, "is it okay if I take about three days off? My end of the paperwork is done, and I need to go to the doctor."

"That takes three days? Yeah, sure, take three days off. Better

□ 185 □

yet, take a week. It can make up for all that overtime, and that way I don't get yelled at."

I don't think that's legal anymore, but I wasn't about to argue. I left fast before he had time to reconsider, and I called my doctor from the pay phone downstairs. After a lot of arguing I convinced the receptionist to let me right on in.

"I'm what?" I said three hours later.

"Let's say Tagamet won't do you a bit of good. You heard me."

"But I can't be," I protested. "I'm forty-two years old! I'm a cop! I'm a *grandmother* even!"

"Tough," the doctor said, grinning at me. "Serves you right for trying to make your own diagnosis. I told you years ago sooner or later this was going to happen."

"Yeah, but I didn't believe you. Okay, what do I do now?"

"Eat right, and that does not mean potato chips and Cokes. Take vitamins. Get enough rest. Come back next month."

"Should I quit jogging?"

He shrugged. "Jog if you want to, unless you get off balance."

Off balance, I thought as I left his office. Off balance? I think off balance.

Harry'll love this.

Captain Millner is going to have cats.

I thought maybe I should wander by the yarn shop and be Knitting Tiny Garments when Harry got home, only I don't know how to knit and if I did, he'd think they were for another anticipated grandchild. So I decided not to buy any yarn just yet, and I thought all the way home of little speeches for different people. I could ask Hal whether he'd like a brother or a sister. I could ask Harry to take me out to dinner and coyly tell him over dessert. I could call Vicky and ask her if I could borrow her maternity clothes. I could ask Becky to hurry up and get married because her room was going to be needed.

No, I had better not do that; she might think I meant it.

I would . . .

Harry was in the front yard raking leaves. Leaving the car door open, barely managing not to trip over Pat, I oozed around the yard broom to fling myself into his arms and scream, "Harry, we're going to have a *baby*!"